A HELPING HAND

CELIA DALE

A Helping Hand

faber and faber

This edition first published in 2008
by Faber and Faber Ltd
3 Queen Square, London WC1N 3AU

A CIP record for this book is available from the British Library

ISBN 978-0-571-24423-2

Mrs Maisie Evans came into the lounge, pulling down the cuffs of her cardigan. 'She's gone, poor soul.'

'Mm? What's that?' Her husband started from the doze into which he always fell immediately after breakfast, the newspaper before his face, waiting for the interior message which, in ten minutes or so, would send him along the

'She's gone. Quite peaceful.' She crossed to the window and drew the curtains so that the sunlight no longer fell on Josh or the colours of carpet and tapestry footstool.

He sank back, crushing the newspaper untidily against his paunch. 'Poor soul. Poor old soul.'

'It was a blessed release·'

'Yes. Yes, I know that. Still, just the same, when it comes. . . .'

'It comes to us all, sooner or later.'

It was a nice morning. From the London Road the sound of traffic had settled into its daytime murmur, and across a sky which was May now although it might revert to March later on, a Caravelle from some far city screeched down on London Airport. If the window had been open Mrs Evans would almost have fancied she smelled blossom, although none was out yet.

Behind her, Josh was wiping his eyes, but put the handkerchief away sheepishly when his wife turned towards him. 'I'll go for the doctor, shall I?'

There's no hurry. 'She looked at the clock on the mantel-piece.' He'll be doing his Surgery now. It's only a formality, after all.'

'Is she . . . ? Do you need any help?'

'I'll get the breakfast things washed up first.'

The television set stood on a low cupboard, the bottom half of a sideboard from which the top had been removed in order that it should better suit the small bright bungalow into which they had moved three years ago. Mrs Evans went to it now and with a little grunt bent down and opened the doors. Half the shelves were neatly stacked with women's maga-zines, knitting and embroidery patterns, and two volumes entitled respectively *The Home Doctor* and *The Home Lawyer*. On the other shelves were Mrs Evans's sewing-basket, knitting-bag and embroidery frame, on which was a half-finished garden scene of a cottage and crinolined lady, destined for a tea-cosy. There was also a shabby leather dressing-case marked with the initials F.B.B.

Mrs Evans lifted this out and set it on the table, and fishing at the neck of her jumper brought out from between her square breasts several keys strung on a chain. With one of these she opened the case and began to check through its contents. Still holding the newspaper, Josh hauled himself out of the chair and came to stand beside her.

There were half a dozen pieces of Victorian jewellery loosely wrapped in yellow tissue-paper, a few yellower photographs. Mrs Evans did not bother with these, but busied herself with documents—Birth Certificate, Insurance Policy, Will. Her grey eyes intent behind her spectacles, she checked each one silently. Beside her, Josh idly picked up a photograph: the girl in it was swathed in serge and lace, waisted like a Christmas cracker. She had a lovely bust. Her hair was looped in wide bay windows either side of her face, which was plain and vary young. Very young.

He put the picture down quickly as his wife stated rather than asked, 'You drew her pension Friday?'

'That's right. As per usual.'

'Give me the book, then.'

He fished in his breast pocket, found it and gave it to her. She put it with the other documents, replaced everything but the jewellery and locked the case, removing the key from the others round her neck and leaving it in the lock.

She was a thickset woman and he a tallish man. She suddenly grinned up at him and punched him lightly on the arm. 'Cheer up, Boy! You look as though you'd lost sixpence and found a penny. Perhaps you'd better get out in the sunshine after all.'

His pink face lightened beneath its silver hair, thick as a cat's fur. 'Shall I go to the doctor, then?'

'May as well. He can please himself whether he comes or not. It's not as if he hadn't expected it. I'll put this in her room.'

She turned and moved briskly to the door, the leather case under her arm, but he still stood by the table. 'You're sure she's. . . ?'

'Don't be soft! Of course I'm sure. You'd better put on your mac, it's treacherous out.'

He heard her in the kitchen, running water for the washing-up, stacking the breakfast crockery. In the shadow of the drawn curtain his chair stood temptingly, the embroidered cushions squashed where he had leaned peacefully against them, a bar of sunlight warming the carpet where his feet had rested. No good going along the passage now, he had missed his moment.

He changed his shoes, walking gingerly past the shut door of the other bedroom, put on his macintosh and hat; then, recollecting, took the hat off again. He opened the kitchen door.

'I'm off, then.'

'Right-o. Don't hurry yourself, it's a nice morning. morning.'

3

'Do you want anything at the shops?'

'No, I'll see to that after the undertaker's been. The doctar'll ring them for you. Tell him she went breakfast-time this morning, very peaceful—say I just found her gone. He can come in after his rounds if he wants to, or he can just make out the certificate straightaway.'

'Okeydoke.'

He closed the kitchen door, tiptoed past the other, let himself out. The sun was warm, the privet was all in bud; it was indeed a lovely morning. Straightening his shoulders, his face falling into its customary folds of innocent good humour, Josh stepped out cheerfully along the road.

2

The plain stretched away below the town's terrace to the rim of the distant sea. The air was so clear that the skyscraper at Cesenatico far to the north could be discerned. The long balcony which is San Marino's town centre seemed to hang in the balmy light, kaleidoscoped by tourists who leaned over its wall, posed against its fountain, clustered before the Town Hall at the far end with its small sentries in green and red. Plodding up the steep streets from the charabancs, the tourists wondered about their hearts, had longed to pause for the placarded 'Tea as Mother makes It', had been unable to catch all the guide's recital of dates and heights and liberties. To emerge on to the terrace was a reprieve and they scattered, light-headed in the limpid air, clicking their cameras, calling to one another in the accents of Manchester, Bermondsey or Berlin, arms, thighs, sometimes even midriffs naked to the warm sun and the cool gaze of the townspeople who passed through them on their own affairs in sober grey or black, or waited within the caverns of their shops, impersonally sharp.

Along the town side of the terrace the tablecloths at the cafés flapped in the breeze. In the shade of the awnings waiters in white coats teased the dogs that came and went among the tables, gossiping against the radio which poured out music and commercials without pause. The tourists sat in the sun; not many of them, for most were either trudging upward again towards the Cathedral and the castles or were ensnared by the shop windows or by refreshments reassuringly advertised (FISH

& CHIPS, TEA STRAIGHT FROM THE POT) . But Josh Evans sat in the sun cm the terrace, his knees comfortably spread, his Italian beach hat on the chair beside him so that he could enjoy the warmth on his head. His short-sleeved shirt, worn outside his trousers and masking his paunch, was open at the neck, showing the skin reddened by the sun, as were his arms. The natural pink-ness of his face had tanned already; from behind his sunglasses he watched the people going to and fro, the old women in their shawled black, the girls decent in their jerseys, the young men, black-spectacled, collared and tied; and the macaw-bright, roast-fleshed tourists. He was absolutely content.

So content that not until his wife was almost at the table did he hear her voice, turning with a start and a smile towards it.

'Ah, here he is,' she was saying, 'sitting in the sun as usual. He's a proper salamander, that's what he is.'

'A salamander? Whatever's a salamander?' A tall woman walking beside her spoke.

'A salamander's what my hubby is, a proper sun-worshipper.' Her jolly laugh was close in his ear. 'Stir yourself, Josh, these ladies are joining us. Where will you sit, dear? I'd get in the shade if I was you after that little turn.'

Josh hoisted himself to his feet, pulled chairs, gathered up and rearranged belongings. There were two women with Maisie, a tall young one—well, young to Josh at sixty, in her thirties somewhere—with severe hair and a nice bust, and an old one Maisie had held by the arm, who walked bow-legged as old people do, with white hair wisping under a raffia hat tied on with ribbon, a beach hat, and a beach hat for a young person at that. Beneath it a small crinkled face pouted and blew, and a gnarled hand pressed against the chest, the other grasping a handbag like a portmanteau.

'That's right, you sit down in the shade and take it easy. My word, it's a climb to the top and no mistake! You knew a thing or two when you chose to stay here, Josh—trust him for

6

that, he's a real fly one—but I must say it's a real panorama when you do get there, see for miles. They say you can see right to Yugoslavia on a really clear day, fancy that now, right across the ocean! Now then, Josh, get the waiter.'

'Yes. Yes, of course. Here—camerary!

'Him and his Italian! He will try it though I tell him they all understand English. What's that stuff you're drinking—coffee? I'll have a cup of tea.'

The ladies agreed, the order was given. They looked about them, at the passers-by, at the Town Hall's pinnacles, at each other.

'Well,' said Mrs Evans, 'this is nice. Are you feeling better now?'

The old lady bridled. 'There's nothing wrong with me. I only need to get my breath.'

'She should never have come,' said the younger woman, 'I told her.'

'I'm independent. I can please myself.'

'What about pleasing other people for a change? I told you you'd never manage it.'

'They should have warned us,' the old lady said sulkily.

'It's on a mountain, isn't it? It's bound to be steep, if you use your brains.' She controlled herself, opening her handbag, and began to wipe her face and neck angrily with a handkerchief.

'It is steep, though,' said Mrs Evans. 'Coming up in the coach, I thought we'd never get round some of those corners. That's one thing I will say for them, they can drive their coaches.'

'And the motorbikes,' ventured Josh.

'Oh, those motorbikes! Tearing about on them at all hours like cowboys!'

'I like them,' said the old lady. They're modern.'

'I like a coach,' said Mrs Evans. There's something solid

7

about a coach and you can look about you and see the country-side. We wondered if we'd book all the way by coach but in the end we decided we'd come by air and just do the excursions by coach. It's more of a break that way, and we'd had a little windfall, as a matter of fact, so we decided to be extravagant. Are you ladies with a coach?'

'We've a car.'

The younger one snapped, 'We've hired a taxi. Auntie has to be able to stop somewhere every other minute.'

'We're with Foodoose Tours,' continued Mrs Evans smoothly. 'We're very satisfied. They look after everything for you but don't get after you all the time, not like some where you never get a minute's peace. There's a nice young chap comes round every evening to see we're all satisfied.'

'We're on our own,' said the young woman, 'which means yours truly has to do all the work.'

'You must let my hubby here do some of it for you. He loves working things out with maps and timetables, don't Boy?'

The waiter brought their tea and a plate of unordered choco-late sweetmeats. Looking warily at her companion from under her raffia brim, the old lady took two and began to eat them quickly.

Her name was Mrs Cynthia Fingal and her niece was Lena Kemp. They were staying in Rimini, while the Evanses were two or three miles up the coast at Salvione, one of the string of holiday places which stretch in an unbroken fringe of concrete, rubble and flowering trees along the edge of the Adriatic sands. Miss Kemp lived in Reading, and, since the death two years ago of a younger aunt, Mrs Fingal had come to live with her. Last year they had gone to Devon for their holiday and had only four sunny days. This year Mrs Fingal had been deter-mined on the sun.

'And we've found it,' she said, looking out over the terrace sparkling high above its sea of space, 'I told you, Lena. I've been here before, with my husband. I remembered the sun. Just after the war, it was—the Great War, of course. His firm sent him and I came too. Not here, but Milan, just after the Great War. I remembered the sun and the lovely peaches. Lena wouldn't believe me.'

'I believed you all right. It's just that things are different when you get to your age.'

'We've never been before,' said Mrs Evans. 'We went to the Costa Brava a few years back, but truth to tell, we haven't been able to manage a holiday for a while, have we, Josh? We've been looking after an old lady, you see, a dear old soul, wasn't she; Auntie Flo we always called her though she wasn't any relation really, just an old lady with no one of her own, so Josh and me took her to live with us.'

'And glad to do it,' murmured Josh.

'Yes, well, poor Auntie Flo, she passed on in March, so Josh and me thought we'd like to get away for a bit of a break, give ourselves a little pick-me-up in the sun. We've been here four days, and I must say, bar that thunderstorm Tuesday evening, the weather's been lovely, hasn't it?'

It's the sun. I remembered it from when my husband and I were in Milan. Just after the Great War, that was, but things don't change all that much, whatever people say.'

Josh leaned forward and tapped his wife on the arm. 'Look at the time, Mai.' They both looked up at the clock beneath the three saints on the Town Hall facade. 'We're going to miss that coach if we don't stir ourselves.'

'My word, so we are!' She began to collect cardigan, handbag, scarf.

Miss Kemp said, 'We could give you a lift back to Rimini if you'd like?'

That's very kind of you, but we'd better stay with the coach. We've got our tickets and all, and it takes us right back to our hotel. Perhaps well run into each other again.'

'That would be nice. It's nice to have someone of your own sort to talk to.'

'We thought of going into Rimini cm Saturday, didn't we, Josh?'

'We could look you up. up.'

'Have a cup of tea somewhere, perhaps?'

There's plenty of places—if you can call it tea, messing about with little bags!'

The Evanses stood up. 'Why don't we pick you up at your hotel,' she said, beaming down at them, the sun making a nimbus of her wiry hair, 'Say about half past three—you'll have had your siesta by then.'

On Saturday. We're at the Miramare—it's right on the main road as you come in from the north, the buses go right past it. The noise!'

'We'll find it. That will be nice. My word, we must run!' She started off down the terrace. Josh raised his hat. 'Ciao!' he said and left them smiling.

The Albergo Garibaldi, not quite an hotel but rather more than a pensionc, stood on the corner of the road leading from Salvione's main street down to the beach. It had been built only two years before and it would be hard to say whether the cracks and crumblings of its structure were signs of incomplction or premature decay. Small trees, coated in the white dust of Salvione's side roads, had been left in a shivering fringe around it, and their shade, and huge dry pots of lilies and geraniums, made the verandah fronting the main road a pleasant place when the sun was too hot for the beach. There were wicker chairs and tables, and here Maisie liked to sit and knit and Josh liked to take his capuccino after lunch and his Campari before dinner and watch the people going up and down the pavements. Everyone whose hotel did not actually front the sea had to go along this road to get to it, and the display of limbs and beachwear was almost as great as if he had been seated under his umbrella in Row D of Bagnio Luigi, the sea a placid glimpse through a metropolis of deck chairs. For fifty miles the sands stretched, but where it fronted Salvione and the other holiday resorts you could see hardly more than you were actually sitting on for the spilliken heap of chairs, towels and bodies, murmurous with transistors, the cries of itinerant ice-cream sellers, the radio aboard the sailing-boat in which you could buy a trip to the horizon, and the squeals of English girls assailed amid the legs of chairs and holidaymakers by Italian beach boys. In every possible shape the human body was revealed, from bikinied girls pliant as daffodils to old men and women whose body hair had turned white; and with the addition of no more than a shirt, most of them walked at least twice a day past the Albergo Garibaldi along the dappled pavements which, when it rained, became lakes of muddy water.

The verandah was used by the Albergo's residents as a café, for most of them were elderly (Footloose enquired your age-group on their registration form and channelled the younger ones to places like Cesenatico, which had plenty of night-life) and did not care to walk or sit too much in the sun. They breakfasted there—there was no space in the bedrooms for room service—and took their casual beverages there, served from the dining-room within the glass doors. Inside these doors could sometimes be seen the proprietress, a woman of iron wrapped in an overall, scrutinising her clients as, long ago, she had scrutinised the pigs and poultry on her father's farm in the foothills of the Apennines. And through these doors, from eight in the morning until ten or eleven at night during the four months of Salvione's season, with two hours off in the afternoon, went the waitresses, Graziella and Francesca, and Alfredo, the boy.

Francesca was sometimes irritable (although she concealed it if the Signora were watching), for her husband gave up work during the season and loafed in the pin-table cafés or along the sands, relying on Francesca's earnings till the Albergo closed again and they both went back to work in the ceramic factory for the winter. Alfredo, who was not yet fifteen, had started work in the Gasthaus Lorelei last year and, although polite enough, did not really wish to understand anything but German. But Graziella, although by evening the skin seemed to lie more thinly on her bones, was always sweet-tempered. She dealt kindly with everyone, the women as well as the men, and was as ready to teach Italian words as to practise her English.

'Buon giorno,' she would smile, bringing their rolls and jam in the morning. 'You sleep very well?'

'Yes, thank you,' they would answer, or 'Not too well, no, there were a lot of lads larking about on their motorbikes,' and she would say, 'Today is very fine, I think. You go on coach?' or, compassionately, 'That is bad. Italian men like very much make too much noise.' Whatever she said, you felt better for it

Josh liked watching her. He liked watching any girl, from the ones on the beach with nothing to cover them but two little strips of stretch nylon, to the hairdressers in the shop over the road, lounging outside the doorway during the slack hours of the siesta, with their bare feet in mules, their hair hugely puffed above their sallow faces, and their bodies surely naked beneath the smocks? They reminded Josh of kittens whose fur was not yet thick on their skins; he could sense them under his palms. He liked to watch Francesca, too, bare heels slapping over the tiles and the strings of her apron going ding-dong with the swing of her buttocks, especially when she was cross. One morning she was very cross and had a bruise on her neck which Josh did not think the other Footloose members would recognise, although you never could tell.

Francesca was more fun to watch, but Graziella gave him

greater pleasure. She was younger, only nineteen, delicate-boned as a bird, and when he saw the alabaster windows in Galla Placidia's tomb in Ravenna one coach trip they took, it made him think of Graziella's face, honey-coloured yet glowing. When she brought him his Campari that evening, while Maisie was upstairs changing her dress, he had tried to tell her.

'La fenestra—Galla Placidia—e come—voi.'

'Come. . . ?'

'Like you—the windows. The light coming through.'

She smiled, showing small, crooked teeth, uncomprehending. He lifted his hand near her face, sketching the line of her cheek. She stood back a little.

'Your face—same colour—colore similare . . .'

Still smiling, she had shaken her head. Francesca paused as she flapped past and Graziella said something to her in Italian. Francesca looked at him out of the corner of her eyes, answered something sharp and went on her way. Josh's eyes went with her apron strings. She had a nice bust, too.

He was talking to Graziella while waiting for Maisie to come down and catch the half past two bus to Rimini for their appointment with Mrs Fingal and Miss Kemp. Maisie liked a cup of tea after her lunch, but forwent it when they were going on a trip because of the hazards surrounding the finding, and condition of, ladies 'lavatories, but Josh liked his Capuccino and Graziella had brought it to him. He was the only one on the terrace. The Signora was eating her lunch in the kitchen while supervising the washing-up of the luncheon crockery and most of the guests were in their rooms or dispersed to beach or outings. Graziella set the cup before him.' Ecco, signor.'

He started out of the light doze that always fell on him after a meal. 'Ah, thank you—grazie.'

'Prego.'

'Grazie—Graziella. Your name.'

She smiled. 'Si, my name. But not "thank you", I think, in Inglese?'

'Miss Thankyou, eh?'

'No, I think more—plain.'

'Grace, is it?'

'I think.'

'Gracie. That's pretty—bella.'

'No, no.' She was laughing, straightening chairs, flicking tables with her napkin.

'Si, si. Graziella e bella.'

She withdrew to a further table. 'You drink. Is going cold.'

'Ah, that's right. You put it out of my mind.' He took a sip of the delicious froth. 'Molto bene.'

'You like?'

'Si, si, molto. Mia piacere—cappucino.'

'You speak very well Italian. Soon speak very well.'

'I'd like to.'

'And I Inglese.'

'You speak English a treat. Parlare Inglese bene.'

'No, not In school I learn, here I learn more but no—many?'

'Much. Not much.'

'Much.'

'You come England, I teach you.'

'Ah!' She sighed. 'I want England very much. My father has been England three years.'

'Get away! Where is he, London?'

'No, no, my father die six years.'

'Ah, I'm sorry.'

'My father in war—prisoner.'

'Ah, in the war.'

'Si. He like very much. Aylesbury. You know Aylesbury?'

'Well, I don't know it, I know of it.'

'My father in prisoners' camp three years Aylesbury. I like very much—go Aylesbury.'

'You come to England, I'll take you. Andiamo—Aylesbury —subito.'

'Ah, magnifico! You speak very well!' She clapped her hands and they beamed at one another.

As he and Maisie waited for the bus he told her how Graziella's father had been a prisoner-of-war in England. 'Fancy that.' she answered absently. 'You got returns, did you?' He had, from the transport agency which changed travellers' cheques. They stood in silence, solitary Anglo-Saxons among three or four soberly dressed Italian girls. Funny how they all had little gold rings in their ears, even the babies. Did it hurt, piercing through the rubbery flesh. . . .? It was hot, but a dry heat Too hot for much on the beach yet, so soon after lunch. . . .

'Here it comes,' she said, and he followed her broad beam up the step.

They did not speak for most of the journey, for Josh dozed off again, his hat on his knees, his white head nodding to the bounce of the wheels, and Maisie was thinking. When the increase in the size of the souvenir shops indicated that they were nearing Rimini, she nudged him. He straightened himself, slipping the good humour back on his face.

'I'll take the girl off,' she said, 'you stay with the old lady.'

'Right you are.'

Soon they alighted outside the Hotel Miramare.

The Miramare was grander than the Albergo Garibaldi. It had been built a few more years and the faults in its construction had been repaired. The trees of its garden were large enough by now to shield it somewhat from the traffic which thundered past its entrance, from Venice down to Bari, and on the other side a terrace set with umbrellas and potted plants, bougainvillea and wisteria, looked out over a gravelly garden to the sands and the sea. A porter in white gloves and braided cap was almost always on duty in the hall, even though he was only sixteen, and the television set was kept in a room of its own, all plastic and mosaic, like a cell made of brawn. Net blowing along the windowed walls gave the rooms an airy elegance.

The ladies were sitting in the shade on the terrace, and Miss Kemp rose as Josh and Maisie came out. She was wearing a tight pink sleeveless dress which showed off her bust, and if she'd had a bit more powder on and her hair not so tightly rolled up off her face she would have been quite taking. Mrs Fingal was sitting with her knees apart and her feet in plimsolls. She wore a string of bright San Marino beads and the same raffia hat.

Chairs were pushed back, pulled up, rearranged. Josh set his hat on the ground beside him and hoped there were no ants. Mrs Fingal was silent, seeming extinguished beneath her candlesnuffer hat. Miss Kemp ran a bracelet up and down her forearm with that air of irritability which underlay everything about her, and exchanged statements with Maisie about the weather and the menu at lunch. 'It's all messed-up dishes. I can't stand messed-up dishes. Why can't they serve a good plain chop now and again?'

'You can't get the quality, not out of England you can't.'

'And that everlasting spaghetti and stuff—what do they call it, pasta? Nothing but Hour and water if you ask me, it puts pounds on you.'

'That needn't worry you, though.'

'Well . . .' she glanced down at herself complacently with a small jerk of her head, half bridle, half preen. It's back to the roast beef of old England when I get home, I can tell you.'

'You can't beat English cooking in the long run.'

'You ought to try Maisie's apple pie.'

'Get along with you! It's just a knack.'

'Lena can't cook.' Mrs Fingal spoke suddenly, 'All out of tins or the freezer.'

The bracelet went up and down the forearm. 'I'm not going to spend hours in the kitchen when I get back from business. It's all very well if you've got nothing else to do.'

Of course, we're retired, 'said Mrs Evans soothingly,' I was a nurse, you know, but I gave it up when I married. At least, I carried on part-time, giving a hand here and there, special cases and that, it seemed wrong not to with everyone crying out for nurses all the time. But when my hubby retired, I gave that up too—although, of course, I'll always help out a friend. That's why we took Auntie Flo.'

'I can't stand sick people.' Miss Kemp straightened her shoulders so that her bosom rose up like a battering-ram.

'That's natural when you're young.' In the pleased pause that followed this remark Mrs Evans gathered up her belongings. 'Well, I suppose we ought to be moving. I'd like to have a look at the shops, there's not a lot of choice in Salvionc.'

Josh shifted his chair but did not rise. 'I wonder, dear—I wonder if you ladies would excuse me?'

'Excuse you?'

'Well, I know what you ladies arc when you get looking in the shops, and it's so hot. Sitting here in the shade with all this lovely sea in front of us is really a treat.'

She wagged a finger at him. 'You're a wicked lazybones, that's what you are!'

He gave his little-boy smile. 'I know. But it's so pleasant sitting here, getting the breeze. I suppose —' he aimed his smile elsewhere, 'I suppose I couldn't persuade Mrs Fingal to keep me company?'

'Well,' Maisie exchanged a look of patience with the younger woman, 'you can hardly sit here on your own in what isn't our hotel. What do you say, Miss Kemp? Shall we girls go off on our own and leave these lazybones?'

Mrs Fingal hitched herself up in her chair. 'You go off. Go on. I don't want to go traipsing round any more shops.'

'Very well. You two sit here then and have a nice rest. We'll be back about five, in time to catch the bus. Don't get up to mischief now!' Smiling, she turned away. As the two women went indoors Miss Kemp could be heard saying, 'Auntie's not up to it anyway . . .'

'Well,' he said, 'here we arc then.' He turned his chair a little to face Mrs Fingal, relaxing and leaning back.

The old lady's lips were trembling. She took a handkerchief from her handbag and pressed it to her mouth then rolled it into a ball between her knotted fingers. 'She's hard. She's all wrapped up in herself. She knows I hear. But she's hard. Never loved anyone but herself. She's not really my niece.'

'No?'

'No. She's no blood relation. My sister's husband's niece. And she's nearly forty.'

'Get away!'

'Thirty-seven. And what's she got to show for it? A desk and a typewriter and some money in the Building Society, that's all she's got to show for it. She's hard.'

'You mustn't let it upset you.'

'No, I mustn't, must I? I'm independent, I can please myself. After all, we're here, aren't we? She didn't want to come. Doesn't like foreigners, can't see outside herself, you see. But I wanted to come and she could take it or leave it I've been in Italy before, you see, with my husband. Years ago, of course, after the Great War. We were in Milan, for his firm. We saw the "Last Supper". It was in a terrible state, all flaking off. They've repaired it now, they say. I made her go to Ravenna. Those mosaics, Mr—er . . .'

'Evans. Josh Evans.'

'Yes. All those little lambs coming out through the doors and the doves flying about and the little flowers. Life's always surprising you. I never imagined anything done in stones being like those little lambs. Did you?'

'No, I can't say I did.'

'I wouldn't go in the other places. That was enough for me. Those little lambs, like Noah's Ark . . . I'll never forget those, nor the Last Supper. There are some things you never forget, isn't that so, Mr—er . . .'

Yes indeed.'

That's enough for me, I told her. You go on, I'll stay in the car. We hired a car, you see. I can't stand crowds. She makes out it's for another reason, but it's because I can't stand crowds. 'She looked at him slyly, but his face was blamelessly attentive. 'Anyway, I stayed in the car, let her go in those other places on her own, hoping to get spoken to, I expect, all those tales you hear about foreigners.'

'You mustn't believe all you hear.'

'No, you mustn't, must you. But it's always true. Those little lambs . . . I'd heard about them but I never expected anything like that.'

'You missed a treat not seeing the tomb. Some empress's tomb it is, by the cathedral.'

'I heard about that but I wouldn't go in.'

'You missed a treat. There's mosaics there . . .' He sketched a shape with his hand, 'You'd think they were real. There's a couple of doves sitting on a sort of a bowl—all done in stone. And the only light's through alabaster.'

'Alabaster?'

'Alabaster. You wouldn't credit it. There's postcards done of the doves and all, but you just have to see the alabaster.'

There was a pause, Josh contemplating the alabaster, Mrs Fingal contemplating him.

'You're artistic. artistic.'

'Oh now, I wouldn't say that'

'You're artistic. My husband was artistic. When we were in Milan after the Great War we used to go into the cathedral and just sit there, looking about us. No need to speak. He'd just take my hand and give it a squeeze and I'd know what he was thinking. And afterwards we bought postcards and we always chose the same.'

'Have you been alone long, Mrs Fingal?'

'Thirty-four years. Pneumonia.' Josh clicked his tongue. 'Thirty-four years in October. They hadn't the drugs then, you see. I still grieve, Mr—er . . .' She pressed the handkerchief to her mouth again.

Of course, of course. And now you live with your niece.'

'She's not my real niece. She's my sister's husband's niece. I lived with my sister but she died. She was younger than me by five years. Heart, it was, just like that.' Josh clicked his tongue again. 'So then Lena took me.'

'You don't want to live alone.'

'I'd had one or two falls. Otherwise I'd rather be independent.'

'I'm sure Miss Kemp's glad . . .'

'Glad of the money! I pay my way, you see, but she's hard. Never a thought for anyone outside herself.'

'And she's your only relative? No sons daughters?'

'She's not a blood relative. She's common. I shouldn't say it, but she's common. Not a bit like our side of the family. I did have one little daughter but she died. They didn't recognise it, you see, and it burst. Alice, we called her, after my husband's mother. He was very attached to his mother. She was only ten. And you? Have you any children?'

'No, unfortunately· Just the two of us. We married a bit late in life—my wife was nearly forty.'

'You want to be young, for marriage.'

'Well, we don't do so badly.' Under his smile Mrs Fingal smiled, straightening her shoulders and shutting the handkerchief away in her handbag. The sun was moving towards them round the corner of the building, the beach and the limpid sea murmurous in the afternoon light. Josh looked at his watch. Would you care for anything, Mrs Fingal? An ice-cream, a cup of tea?'

'Well, thank you. How kind. They don't have very much here.'

'We could go for a stroll. The strength's gone from the sun a bit now.'

'And go to a café? That would be a treat!'

'We'll play truant together, shall we?' He twinkled at her and she, pulling herself to her feet, twinkled back.

'I must just . . .' I'll just change my hat. And you, perhaps . . .' She gestured vaguely towards the hotel. He gave a small bow.

'I'll wait for you inside.'

She gathered her possessions and trundled away. Following leisurely, Josh found the lavatory: mosaic walls and floor, liquid soap, paper towels, really good style. This hotel was obviously more expensive than the Albergo Garibaldi.

They set out along the dappled pavement, Mrs Fingal clinging to his arm. The traffic rushed closely past them, for the path was narrow and Mrs Fingal, not too steady on her feet, was in fear of being whirled in its slipstream. They proceeded slowly, she on her bent old legs, he with his dignified paunch, pausing now and then to look at the flowers in the grounds of villas and hotels. Soon they found a café with tables set under umbrellas, and Mrs Fingal admired his command of Italian— due cassatti, due capuccini, per favore.

Spooning the ice-cream greedily she said, 'Lena'd be jealous! She doesn't know how to go out with a man.'

'Has she never . . . ?'

21

'She frightens them off. She's not womanly. And at her age they're all married. Or something wrong With them.'

'She's quite a good-looking woman. You'd think . . .'

'She's hard. Wrapped up in herself. Men don't like that. Me sitting here with a man—oh, she will be vexed!'

Roguishly he suggested, 'Perhaps you'd better not tell her?'

'I wouldn't miss her face. I haven't talked to a man—except tradesmen and the doctor, of course—since, oh, I don't know how long. You miss it, you know, you miss the masculine viewpoint if you've been married.'

'And I'm sure you don't need to see the doctor often?'

'Not very often. I have my regular tablets, and I don't get much trouble really. My husband would have been eighty-three.'

'He was older than you by a long way, then.'

She was coy. Only four years.'

'Get away!' She nodded, licking the spoon with smiling lips. 'Well, I'd have given you not a day more than sixty-five.'

'You're just saying that.'

'No, I'm not. Not a day more than sixty-five—sixty-six perhaps.'

'Well—I do keep active, whatever Lena says. It was I who insisted on coming to Italy. She didn't want to. But I'm independent, I can please myself. I always wanted to come back after that time I was in Milan with my husband after the Great War. And as I was paying, I had my way.'

He let her maunder on, sometimes inserting a comment or a question. Under his smiling attention she began to sparkle. She raised her chin as though to lift it clear of the dewlaps, stretched her neck as though it were still the column of creamy flesh on which the head, chestnut dark then, white now, used to ride so gracefully, sending slanting glances that had once ravished. From inside this heap of old flesh peeped a girl, a bride, a young mother, ridiculous and sad. Only half-listening

22

to what she said, Josh registered her flowering. His kind eyes answered hers, although his thoughts were on the three German girls writing postcards at a nearby table, their thighs like copper beneath their shorts, and on the girl who worked the coffee machine with arms as round and brown as almonds; and he allowed his hand to linger for a moment on Mrs Fingal's elbow after he had eased her from her chair to return to the Miramare. Slowly they walked back. Now it was he who took her arm, to steady her at a rough pavement, to protect her at a crossing, not she his. At his side she danced, and he, carrying his hat, inclined his head towards her so that the sun sparkled its silver, his lips curved in indulgent good humour. He was wondering what he had done with their return bus tickets.

He helped her up the hotel steps. Maisie and Miss Kemp were waiting for them, and Miss Kemp immediately attacked. 'Where on earth have you two been? We've been waiting ages.'

Mrs Fingal ignored her, smiling on Maisie from the shelter of Maisie's husband. 'Did you find what you wanted? I hope Lena didn't drag you too far.'

'You might have left word. We didn't know where you'd got to.'

'I was in good hands.'

Maisie hauled herself up from the settee; her slowness came from solidity, not age. 'You're right enough with my Josh. I'm sure he took good care of you.' She smiled at him and he, with a little bow, smiled back.

'We took a little stroll . . .'

'And had ice-cream. Under umbrellas, out of doors. And I had coffee.'

'You'll suffer for it'

'No I shan't.'

'You'll be up all night groaning. Don't expect me to sympathise.'

23

'I've got my tablets.'

'She knows she can't take coffee. Palpitations, wind. . . .' Why do I bother?'

Josh's face was troubled. 'I'd no idea.'

'Oh, one wouldn't expect a man to think!' Her look was contemptuous but her bust challenged. Countering her gaze with humility, Josh thought all she needed was some rum-tum-tum. Hair scraped back, no make-up, and yet that tight dress. He sighed.

Maisie opened her bag and routed about in it. 'I've got some wonderful powders for indigestion. Our chemist at home makes them up, I never go anywhere without them.'

'Oh, we've got powders! Proper chemist's shop we have to travel with, and if we run out heaven knows what happens, as I told her when she would have it we must come abroad. It's not as if it was just her, it's other people that have the worry. It's other people that have the responsibility.'

Mrs Fingal had shrunk. Her gaze wandered here and there, her head began to shake slightly, and her hands, clutching her handbag to her stomach, trembled. Her lips moved but did not speak.

With smooth words Maisie eased the awkwardness. Tucking her hand under Miss Kemp's arm she drew her to the steps, talking of the bus back to Salvione and of their next meeting. Josh touched Mrs Fingal's elbow gently to follow them.

'She's jealous,' she muttered. That's what it is. She's jealous.'

'You mustn't upset each other. That would spoil what's been a very pleasant afternoon.'

She gathered herself a little. 'It has, hasn't it? She can't take that away. I don't know when I've had such a pleasant afternoon.'

'My sentiments exactly.'

'You don't know what it's like, never having masculine

companionship. Not when you've been married. Thirty-four years in October, but I still grieve. You miss the company'.

'I understand.'

'Do you?' She stared up at him. 'The little attentions—like walking on the outside of the pavement and ordering and knowing which platform. When you've had it you miss it. She wouldn't know the difference.'

He touched her elbow again gently. 'They're waiting for us.'

She nodded, suddenly restored. 'It was a delightful afternoon. She's only jealous.'

She was still standing on the steps, waving vigorously despite Lena at her side, when the bus back to Salvione carried them away.

Once again the Evanses were silent on the journey, but this time it was Maisie whose head jolted in sleep and Josh who looked out over the flat fields edged with trees and seamed with reeded dykes. It was a graceless countryside, a huge allotment rather than farmland, the seashore lying like a rich scum along its edge. Along this back road parallel with the sea there were few tourists, only the inhabitants going secretively about their business, their Vespas and bicycles, bare shops heaped with fruit and vegetables, grocers' windows advertising laxatives and cartoned gnocchi, and the women, sallow and sober, with little chains round their necks from which the gold crosses pointed always downward to what was out of sight.

They nodded to fellow guests who already sat on the Garibaldi's terrace waiting for dinner, and went up to their room.

There was not much space, allowing for bed and wardrobe, in what (perhaps at the Miramarc?) could properly have been a single room, and they had learned to take their activity in turns. When Josh came back from along the passage (there was more oil than he was used to even in the Signora's anglicised cooking) Maisie had washed and was lying on the bed in her petticoat, smoking a cigarette. He shut the door quietly.

25

'Just a Hide bit loose.'

'Want some chloridine?'

'I'll see how I go.' He removed his jacket and hung it over the back of the only chair, then took off his shirt, sniffing it. This warm weather!'

'Be grateful it's drip-dry.'

'That's right. Don't know how they managed before in hot climates.' He turned on the tap marked C and waited a moment, scratching his chest through his singlet. 'The water's cold again. again.'

'It's warmer in the cold.'

The basin filled with brownish water and he began to wash, sluicing his face and neck with energetic noises. When, puffing, he was drying himself, Maisie said, 'Well?'

'She's a dear old soul.' Maisie waited. 'She's footing the bill.'

'I know that.'

'I don't think there's a lot. A sanitary engineer, her hubby was—wash-basins, WC's. He passed away a long time ago, but the old girl speaks very touchingly of him, very touchingly indeed. Close your eyes, dear, I'll just have a wash.' She closed her eyes, drawing on the cigarette, and Josh peeled off the singlet and washed his chest and armpits. 'She pays for her board with the niece.'

'Not much.'

'She thinks so. There's no love lost. Makes out it was only that that made her niece take her in. It sounds likely to me.'

'Yes, of the two. She's not her real niece, only by marriage.'

That's right.'

'No one else?'

'Doesn't seem so. She had a little girl but she died, poor little soul.'

Maisie opened her eyes as Josh pushed the vest back round his soft pink belly, and stubbed out her cigarette. 'I think they might do, 'she said, and swung her feet down off the bed. 'We'll have to see.'

The two couples saw a great deal of one another. Not more than a day or two passed without some visit or excursion. For short distances Mrs Fingal hired a taxi and they all went, but for longer journeys she was left in Rimini with Josh for company. Even on the shorter expeditions the two younger woman tended to go off together, up the towers, down the dungeons where the crowds pressed in and were bad for Mrs Fingal's heart. The short, broad street that led, for instance, from Gradara's gate up to its castle she could manage, clinging to Josh's arm; but the winding steps by which one entered were too much for her. She and Josh retired, leaving Maisie and Miss Kemp squeezed among the half-naked bodies of other tourists, battered by their multiple languages and by the Italian radio which maintained its vivacious flow from every café clustered outside the castle walls. It was certainly more agreeable to saunter out along the lane that ran outside the battlements, to sit in the shade, the terracotta walls rearing behind one to their fishtail crests, and look out across a pastoral land rimmed by the sea. The air smelled of leaves, there were no cars or petrol fumes; even the radios could not be heard here, nothing but the trees moving in the soft air, the far chink of a pail, a goat's bleat. If he had been alone, he would have dozed off till Maisie fetched him, but Mrs Fingal was, as usual, there. Although his mind slept behind his open eyes, her presence required certain things: the kindly smile, the right interpolation. For she talked almost all the time and most of it he didn't listen to, only a detail here and there, building up the picture Maisie wanted, and for the rest dozing on the quiet hillside, enjoying the peace. Until Mrs Fingal grew anxious about the coldness of the stone on which they sat and he had to stir himself and take her back.

'Some people know how to take things easy,' said Miss Kemp aggressively, 'although I must say you didn't miss much. All that stuff about Paolo and Francesca—it's just put out for the tourists.'

Miss Kemp's view of foreigners was uncompromising. Anything that was passably satisfactory on the Adriatic coast was done better in Torquay, where she had spent three successive holidays before Mrs Fingal had been wished on to her. Wished on to her by whom? Mrs Evans delicately probed. Well, no one really —Auntie herself; there was no one else.

'How sad!' sighed Mrs Evans.

'Oh, Auntie's kind always find someone soft enough to look after them. She's been spoiled all her life—first her husband, then Auntie Peg. She doesn't know what it is to stand on her own feet.'

'It's a great thing to have a training, like you and me. I mean, you're a professional woman, you can make your own way any day. And, well, if anything were to happen to my hubby, there's all my nursing experience I could fall back on.'

The two women were in Florence. It was their day-long, last excursion before the Evanses returned home. Josh should have spent the day with Mrs Fingal, but when Maisie joined the coach in Salvione, thumping down into the seat which Lena had kept for her, she had announced that Josh was poorly. 'Nothing serious, just a little tummy upset.'

'It's all that oil they cook with. Oh lor, I suppose I ought not to come. Heaven knows what Auntie'll get up to on her own all day.'

'Well, it's too late now, dear.' Nose towards the foothills, the coach had been irrevocably on its way. 'Don't worry, she'll be all right. One of the waitresses promised to phone her and explain why he wasn't coming–she speaks quite good English. He was upset to have to let us down like this, and so was I.'

Indeed, she had been. She had stood at the bedside with her jaw squared, glaring down at a Josh, who lay against the pillow saying feebly, 'I daren't, Mai. I daren't go more than two steps away from the toilet.'

She had left him with chloridine and Beecham's Powders, organised Graziella to telephone the Miramare and take him some weak tea, and stumped out to catch the coach. 'I wasn't going to have our last outing spoiled,' she had patted Lena's hand. 'Besides, it's already paid for.'

They had chatted, stared out at the shifting landscape as the coach twisted up into the mountains, half heard the courier's inadequate information, half dozed against the background of radio and static which the driver never gave up hope of blending. At an albergo at the highest point of the route they had taken in and let out liquid. They had kept themselves to themselves and strolled the other way when the albergo's car park had been filled with an avalanche of Germans from another tour. They had stretched their stiff knees along the palisades of the Piazza Michelangelo, the rosy breasts of Florence awaiting them in the haze below, and smiled 'Cheese' to the photographer who made his living recording each coach load. They had been herded through the gorgonzola opulences of the de Medici tomb, through the Cathedral, the Baptistery, never quite hearing all the courier said, always half hearing the French, Italian, German buzz of other couriers who circled and gave jealous room to rival flocks, like testy sheepdogs. They had sweated along narrow streets, between walls like fortresses, over broken pavements, among the rasp of motor-cycles. They had been abandoned in the Piazza Signoria, awash with fiacres and the huge limbs of statues, and told to reassemble four long hours hence—four hours, how could they fill four hours!— and now sat among the pigeon droppings under the colonnade of the Uffizi, the stone bench cool through their cottons, furtively consuming their packed lunches.

'I mean, nursing is something that's always of value, like a good business training.' She bit efficiently round a chicken bone. 'I feel sorry for someone who hasn't got something like that to fall back on.'

'You needn't feel sorry for Auntie. She's well taken care of.'

'I'm sure she is. You must be such a comfort . . .'

'I was soft. I could kick myself. She's not got all that much, but there must be old people's homes where people like her are looked after.'

'Was it suggested?'

'Well, it was and it wasn't. She couldn't run to a private place, and the Government places—well, you have to be destitute, more or less. How do they expect you to eat a peach if they don't give you a knife to peel it with?'

'Break the skin with your teeth.'

'And get typhoid—no thank you!' She began to scratch at the peach with her fingernail, and the juice ran down her knuckles and dripped on to the paper napkin in her lap. 'When Auntie Peg died she was all upset—you know, shakey and having her palpitations but not bad enough for a hospital, and like a fool I said I'd have her for a week or two till she found somewhere to go. That's over two years ago and she's still there.'

'Still, you're not out of pocket, are you?'

'It's the inconvenience. Just because she pays for her board she feels it's her home. What she pays me doesn't make up for the inconvenience of always having her under my feet. It's not as though she'd stay in her room. I can't have my friends in without Auntie bustling in and gassing on about when she was married and all that.'

'I don't suppose they mind.'

'Well, my girl friends have to put up with it, but I can't ever invite a man. You know what men are, always have to be the centre of the stage.'

Maisie tapped her playfully on the arm. 'Ah ha, so there's a gentleman friend, is there?'

A blush ran up, from her neck to the roots of her severely rolled back hair. 'I can't be bothered with men.'

'A fine-looking girl like you . . .'

'All men want is a pretty face. They don't want a woman with brains, it makes them feel small. A pretty face to go to bed with, that's all men want.'

'The right type of man, dear—and he does exist—has more sense than that. The right type likes someone he can talk to, share his business troubles with, and find attractive, too.'

'I've got something better to do than go around looking for men.' She gathered the picnic debris into a pile and thrust it into the carrier bag. Maisie took out a handkerchief and began to wipe her greasy lips and fingers. The pause lasted quite a long time. Then in a distant voice Lena said, 'But there is this man at the office I sometimes have a drink with after business. He's married, of course—I don't know what his wife thinks when he's half an hour late home. Not that she need think anything, we only just happen to meet in the local.'

'It's a friendly habit, that. After business, a chat over a drink —relaxing.'

'Yes.' Sidelong, she caught a sidelong glance from Maisie.

'Yes,' Maisie echoed reflectively.

They began to tidy everything away, throwing a crust or two to the pigeons. Maisie rose and shook her dress into place. 'So really you'd like to find somewhere where your auntie could be looked after, paying her way, of course—like dear old Auntie Flo did with me and my hubby.'

'Oh, I would! It'd be worth almost anything to me to get her off my neck.'

'I wonder. . . .' Neat and broad, she stood in the shadow of the colonnade as solid and grey as a statue, her eyes almost shy behind their spectacles. 'You see, we've still got Auntie Flo's room. . . .'

When the door shut behind his wife, Josh lay listening to his gastric juices running up and down. Occasionally a gripe took him, so mild as to be almost pleasurable. His intestines felt agreeably scoured out by the trip along the passage which he had been forced to make soon after six o'clock that morning and which, if he knew his own insides, would probably be the only one. When he saw, from the watch on the chair beside the bed, that Maisie must definitely be on the coach by now, he sank down under the bedclothes, turned on his side, and was fast asleep in an instant.

When he awoke the shutters had been closed, his dressing-gown neatly laid at the bottom of the bed, and a tray bearing a glass of lemonade and a packet of biscuits left on the chair. He heaved himself up, happiness overwhelming him. The day stretched around him like the bed, warm, friendly, and empty of everyone but himself. Today would be his holiday; no Maisie, no blithering Mrs Fingal, just himself and all the beauties of the beach and cafés, the hairdressers and the shops.

He put on his dressing-gown and slippers and went along the passage. As he had thought, the storm had blown itself out. He felt very well, very well indeed—so well that he carefully brushed his hair and cleaned his teeth (most of them were his own) and dabbed a little After-Shave round his jaw before getting back into bed to munch the biscuits and wait for who-ever was coming to fetch the tray.

It was Graziella. 'Ah signor—you are better?'

'Un poco. Mai a stomaco.' He patted it wanly.

She came into the room, leaving the door open. 'Many Ingles people have bad stomach. Is different kitchen, yes?' Her face was full of tenderness and concern. 'You have hunger?'

'Perhaps—un poco. I don't know if I have a fever.'

She came to the bedside and laid her fingers on his forehead. 'Is cold—no fever.'

He caught her hand as she withdrew it and gazed winningly up at her. 'Was it you —who bring —limonade?'

'Si. When finish la prima colazione, I come. You sleep, come un bambino.'

'You should have woken me up.'

'Ah no, for stomach sleep very good.' She gently disengaged her hand and picked up the tray, stepping back from the bedside. 'Signora Evans say telephone Hotel Miramare in Rimini and this I do. I speak with manager and he speak the signora. Now—you eat?'

He let his head droop back against the pillow. 'Perhap —a little soup.'

'Bene.'

She had gone before he could say anything more, but he practised phrases in his head as he awaited her return, thumbing through the pocket dictionary he kept by him.

'Ecco!' She steadied the door with her foot, then brought the tray to the bed.

'Ah, grazie—grazie, Graziella, eh?' Smiling, he heaved himself upright.

'Prego.' From the neck of her dress her gold cross hung forward as she laid the tray on his lap. 'You eat—good for stomach.'

He patted his stomach ruefully. 'Too much stomacho—troppo!'

'Ah no—you eat.' Her eyeteeth were a little crooked but very white. 'Make you strong.'

'I not strong. I very weak. You feed me—like un bambino?'

She smiled down at him. 'You not bambino. You Signor Evans.'

'Poor old Signor Evans.'

'No, not poverino. Please, you eat.' Grudgingly, he began the soup, 'Is good?'

'Si, si.' It was a thin broth with vermicelli, not a patch on the tinned soup Maisie gave him. 'In Inghilterra we have—zuppa—molto . . .' he sought for the word in the air with the spoon, 'molto thick.'

'Thick?'

'Si—duro.' She frowned. 'Thick—non come acqua, come —come crema.'

'Ah, si. We also. But for stomach, this.'

'You come Inghilterra—visit Aylesbury—I give you English soups, yes?'

'Yes? I like very much visit Aylesbury.'

'You come, then. I'll look after you.'

'I hope, one day.'

'You come subito—visit poor old Signor Evans.'

Her glance was grave. 'I think you have—il cuore d'un ragazzo.'

'Cuore?'

'Si.' She pressed her clasped hands to her breast. 'Here, I think—like a boy, no?'

'Heart?'

'Si.' Her smile flashed as she went to the door. 'So, you eat.'

He stared at the door, a pleasurable glow warming his spirit as well as his body. The heart of a boy, eh? What a turn of phrase these Italians had! Il cuore d'un ragazzo . . . 'like a melody, cuore. . . .' He finished the broth, vermicelli and all, and the roll, dry though it was, for he was hungry. He could have done with a peach but perhaps fruit wasn't wise just yet Anyway, there wasn't one. He would get up presently and go and have a coffee and cakes in the main street But not yet. She had to come back for the tray yet He sank a little down under the bedclothes and watched the door.

It was not she but Francesca. She bounced in, demanding,

'Finito, signor?' her eyes sharp round the room. The tower of her hair sagged a little, for they had just finished serving lunch and she had been at work since seven-thirty.'

'Ah si—finito, grazie.'

'Prego.' She came to the bedside and picked up the tray. 'Va migliore stomaco?'

'Migliore?'

With her free hand she patted her apron. 'Stomaco—very good?'

'Ah si—very good,' and he slid his hand up her skirt.

He had time to feel the hairs on the back of her thighs, the edge of her briefs, the moist crease of her buttock within, before she gave a scream and leaped away, the plates sliding on the tray. He stared up at her innocently as she upbraided him; the only word he recognised was 'cattivo' but he got her drift. She bounced to the door, tossing her head indignantly, and slammed it behind her.

Well, it had been worth a try. His fingers smelled of her. He would think about it a little before he got up.

He went downstairs and out on to the terrace, cautiously, for it would probably be best not to run into her until she'd had time to cool off. The dining-room was empty and there was only one elderly English couple sitting in the shade of the terrace, she writing postcards, he fast asleep. Josh stood for a moment on the step, settling his Italian hat on his head, pondering which way to go. To the beach, to sit under the umbrella with his legs in the sun, watching the somnolent bodies stretched around him? Or up the main street, to buy a coffee from waitresses idle enough so near the siesta hour to get into conversation with? Or perhaps to have his hair cut, a manicure even, from one of those kitten girls in their nylon shifts? As he pondered, feeling the sun begin to late gently through his shirt, a taxi drove round the corner and

35

stopped in front of him, and out of it clambered Mrs Fingal.

'Oh Mr Evans! What luck! I was afraid—and here you are after all!' Clutching her handbag, she trundled towards him, her face radiant under the raffia hat. 'I didn't know— the porter simply said you were ill and I know how one *can* be—and no one here, so I thought—After all, you might have been really . . .'

He caught her elbow to steady her as she lurched up the steps almost into his arms, his smile adjusting itself to mask the emotions caused by her arrival. 'Why, Mrs Fingal—this is a surprise. . . .'

'Yes, isn't it, but I thought, why shouldn't I, I can please myself and anyway we needn't tell them, and after all, the message did say you were ill.'

'So I was—well, not to say ill, just poorly, you know, a tummy upset. It's the oil, I dare say.' He stood grasping her elbow, making phrases.

"And the fruit. So delicious but we're not really used to it. You don't drink the water?'

'Never touch the stuff.'

'My husband always drilled into me, never touch the water. Being a sanitary engineer, you see, he knew. The things he explained to me about their plumbing, their sewage system! Of course, this is all some time ago, after the Great War.'

'What about the taxi?'

'Oh, that's all arranged. The porter did it, it's his uncle. He's to wait and take me back at six o'clock. Then I'll be back in plenty of time before Lena and she needn't know.'

Releasing her, he glanced at his watch. It was barely three. 'Well,' he said genially, 'you'd better come and sit down.'

Her colour was in patches now and she had difficulty in getting her breath. But her eyes shone as she sat looking round at the dusty plants, the cracked pavements, and at him, pink and white in his short-sleeved shirt and light slacks.

'You're not cross with me?'

'Get away! It's a pleasant surprise.'

'I thought, why shouldn't I? Even if she knew, she can't eat me. I'm independent. And they just said you were ill and I thought, they've gone off and left him and perhaps he's in need. That's what I thought, I thought perhaps he's in need. They wouldn't think, you see—at least, Lena wouldn't. She's just wrapped up in herself, you see, hard, no thought for others, never having been married. And I thought, she'll insist on their going even if he's in need, and Mrs Evans wouldn't like to refuse. And I brought these.' She opened her bag and took out a pillbox. 'There's a chemist shop just near the hotel — farmacista, they call it—and I went in and made myself understood. I thought you might not have anything. Lena says foreign medicines aren't any good, but they're just as intelligent as English people—think of Pasteur and the Curies—such a lovely film, those little lumps glowing there in the dark . . .' She lost the thread, then thrust the box towards him, eager beneath her raffia hat. 'They're for . . .' she whispered, 'diarrhoea.'

He turned the box between his fingers. 'Now that is thoughtful of you, Mrs Fingal—really thoughtful.'

'I know what it is, you see. You don't forget how to look after people, not once you've known. But perhaps you've got some?'

'No, no, nothing like this. These'll put me right in no time.'

'It says on the box when to take them—Italian's quite easy when you know what it's saying. But she won't make the effort. Selfish, you see. Respect for other people's way of life is the hallmark of the gentleman, that's what my husband used to say. Although, of course, he could be very firm. He had to be, so soon after the war—the Great War, that was—and their different ways of looking at sanitation. But of course, that time they were our allies.' She paused, looking round at

37

the somnolent, sunny afternoon with indulgence, 'So they ought always, silly creatures. Don't you think?'

'Yes, yes. Yes indeed.'

'They're like children. Very knowing children. Whatever they do, they do without any shame, just like children, good or bad. Children always follow a bully, don't they—and all that dressing up. Of course, it had hardly started when my husband and I were here, but it doesn't surprise me, not seeing them now. Everything written up in German—you'd think they'd resent them, wouldn't you, after all that happened? I can't talk like this to Lena. She shuts me up. She can't see outside herself, you see. And she's common. There's never any conversation, she hasn't the patience to listen to anyone but herself. I used to talk to my sister a bit, and I had a friend, a Mrs Turner I was at school with, we used to write long letters to each other until her arthritis got too bad. And she's passed away now, of course. But I miss the conversation. My husband and I were never at a loss. We understood each other. I never found the same understanding once I lost him, not even my sister. In fact, we used to quarrel. Sisters do, you know. But she was company too, not like Lena. She's not my real niece, you know, only by marriage.'

It was hard to judge when she expected a response, but he made one now, something about life having its ups and downs. She remained silent, suddenly shrunk down in the chair as though all the vitality had been emptied out of her, clinging to the hasp of her handbag as though to a raft. He glanced sharply at her and saw how pinched and grey she had gone.

'Can I get you something? It's hot out here, perhaps we should go inside. . . .'

'No, no, I like it. It's a dry heat.'

'A cup of tea?'

'Perhaps presently.' She routed about in her handbag and found some pills.

He half rose. 'Some water?'

'No, no. They dissolve—under the tongue, but I always find that so difficult.' She popped one into her mouth and looked at him quite gaily. 'It's you who should be taking pills. You must take care of yourself, you know.'

'I do that all right, never you fear.'

'I know what men are, ashamed to take care of themselves. My husband was the same. He hated being what he called fussed. Don't fuss, Cynthie, he'd say. But you need to be taken care of.'

He looked at his watch. It was only half past three. 'Would you care for a stroll? It's shady in the main street.'

'That would be very nice.'

'There's not much to see.'

There's the shops. And it's such a treat to go for a walk with a man. We never see a man—she puts them off, you see, being so wrapped up in herself. They don't like that. She never brings one home. You miss the little attentions when you've been married.'

They gathered themselves together. He gave her his arm. Bright-eyed, she clung to it. They walked slowly up Salvione's main street, looking in every shop, and Mrs Fingal hardly ever stopped talking. Most of the hairdresser girls were inside and at work, but one leaned against the doorway filing her nails and looked curiously at them as they passed. He caught her black-fanned eye, and held in his paunch as much as the belt of his slacks would allow. The girl's expression did not change but her gaze accepted what he was. When they reached the end of the shops they crossed over and had ice-cream in the café with pin-tables and, at night, a band. A party of Manchester accents was in noisy rivalry over the scoring and some younger English tourists in shorts were doing the Twist to the radio that stood, permanently switched on, behind the Gaggia. Both performances entertained the waiters and it was hard for

Josh to get attention. But it amused Mrs Fingal and passed the time.

Then slowly they walked down the other side of the street, back towards the sea. Although it was still bright, the bite of the sun was going. As it lessened, the pull of the beach relaxed and life began to flow back into the town, sauntering under the little trees, glancing, pausing, loud with many voices, a tide obedient to the sun which in the morning drew it down to the water's edge and in the evening let it roll back into the land again. The townspeople who, in the baked midday hours, had sat outside their shops or done their marketing or cycled busily in the half-empty streets, now withdrew once more into their shops to serve, sallow and hollow-eyed under the weak electric light, until the last postcard, the last foreign newspaper, the last pair of wooden sandals strapped with gold seemed likely to have been sold until tomorrow. Sluggishly the tide eddied past their windows, fingering shirts and beach smocks hung on outside racks, the street loud with exhausts and peremptory hootings, speeding to Rimini, to Cesenatico, to Cervia, drawing the day's heat away from the town.

Slowly, tediously, Josh manœuvred Mrs Fingal through the crowd. She would look at everything, was trying to find a final postcard to complete a set of the mosaics which had so pleased her in Ravenna, but was beginning to reel a little and drag uncomfortably on his arm. He got her at last down to the sandy lane that ran behind the beach, edged for a little way by pine trees set with a few benches, and on one of these she sub-sided, panting slightly. He too was not sorry to sit down; the ice-cream had been unwise and gripes were glancing over his stomach, not bodeful but unpleasant.

'Oh,' she gasped, 'how peaceful it is! And the sea—like silk! Shot silk.'

The sand and the sea lay together, silver-gilt in the late after-noon light. Along the beach the deck chairs were already being gathered and snapped shut by the attendants, the umbrellas furled. There were still bathers, still braised bulky people playing beach ball, uttering shrieks, still a child or two screaming as its parent rinsed it, squirming, under the fresh-water tap. Somewhere an ubiquitous radio spoke of soap. But space and silence waited, almost in sight.

He placed his hat on the bench beside him, took out a handkerchief and wiped his forehead, careful not to disarrange his hair. 'There's a nice breeze here.'

'Don't catch a chill. It's very treacherous. You could easily catch pneumonia, and with your little upset. . . . You mustn't take risks, I'd never forgive myself.'

'How about you, Mrs Fingal? We mustn't let any harm come to you either.'

'Oh, me . . . !' She made a confused gesture. There's no need to worry about me. I'm of no consequence. That's made plain enough every day when I'm at home. For a time I gave up. When my little girl was taken—she was only ten. But I had my husband then, of course, and he gave me the strength. Are you a religious man?'

He met her gaze warily. 'I believe there is One Above.'

'Do you? Do you indeed? You may be right. But it hardly seems relevant, does it? I mean, divine will and so on, so quite incomprehensible, you'd think we could be given a glimpse, some hint of what. . . . As it is, one can't fathom it, why he should take a little girl of ten and leave so many useless old people. And all the divorces, murders even, and others not spared. . . .'

'God works in a mysterious way.'

'Yes. Yes indeed. Sometimes quite wonderfully, of course· Like our meeting.'

'Yes, that was a happy chance and no mistake. mistake.'

'Do you feel that? It could only have been chance, of course, because I don't really believe in anything being meant, do you

41

—but there, you do, you're a believer. But to me it was simply a happy chance, as you say, but such a happy one. Such a happy one.'

'It was certainly happy for us.'

'Was it? For you too? You feel that? Your wife and Lena getting on so well, and you and me. . . . Our little walks and our talks—such companionship, such understanding, and the little attentions only a man . . . I can't tell you, I can't tell you. . . . You think you get used to it, but you don't. And to think you leave tomorrow.'

Her hands flurried here and there over her handbag and her head began to shake a little. Her trembling and his silence lay for a moment between them before he reached out and laid one of his hands upon hers. 'But this won't be the end of the chapter. We'll see one another again.'

'Shall we?' Under his hand hers stilled. 'It would mean so much. But the journey—Reading's so awkward. I couldn't expect . . .'

'You could come and visit us. We could put you up. We've still got Auntie Flo's room. . . .'

When Maisie got back that evening Josh was already in bed. He laid the paperback down on his neatly folded sheet. 'Had a good day, did you?'

'I think so.' She sat and took off her shoes, then started to undress. 'She made the offer.'

'Ah.' He averted his eyes as the petticoat peeled off and she turned her broad, corseted back. 'I had a bit of luck too.'

'Luck?'

'The old lady. She turned up here.'

'Here? What, up here in the bedroom?' Slipping the night-dress over head, she faced him again.

'No, downstairs. I felt a bit better after lunch and had a bit of a sit on the terrace. She turned up in a taxi.'

'Well, I never!'

'She doesn't want Lena to know, poor old soul. But she made the offer too.'

Husband and wife looked at each other, the slow smile on her face drawing one to his. She reached forward and struck him lightly on the arm. 'That's my Boy,' she said, before turning to the wash-basin to rinse her dentures.

EW ANMIE,
                                    Greenlea Avenue,
                                        Ellbrook, M'sex.

Mia cara 'Gracie',

Come sta? Io sono bene ma non abiamo molto sol in Inghilterra adesso.

Enclosed as promised are the snaps I took. The one of you smiling is nice but the others do not do you justice. The one with Francesca in as well is a good souvenir of a happy holiday although Francesca is looking a bit old-fashioned I (This is an English way of saying she looks a bit angry.) I hope her husband has not been playing her up!

We had a good journey back and found everything here all right. The weather is not too good but after sunny Italy I should not complain. I wonder how you and all at the Albergo Garibaldi are? I should like to hear from you and of course it would be good practice for your English. As you can see, I have not got far with my Italian I So please drop me a line. And remember you promised to come and see us here one day and we will make that visit to Aylesbury! I mean it. It would be a real pleasure to see you here any time.

Remember me to all at the Albergo and hoping to hear from you. A riverderci!

                                    Yours very sincerely,
                                        Joshua Evans.

My dear Mr Evans,

Just a line to say I hope you and Mrs Evans arrived home safely and that the journey was not too bad. The glorious weather broke just after you left—perhaps it was an omen!— and we made our departure in torrential rain and a thunder-storm, really most dramatic, but the airport people were quite unperturbed, indeed almost careless, and although I expected to be struck by a Bolt from the Blue at any moment, all was well and as the saying is, we rose above it. Lena was a bit windy which made her very crotchety, and did not take Kindly to my suggestion that if we were going to meet our Maker we were a good many thousand feet nearer Heaven than we should be going by train! She has no sense of humour.

The flat here seems very dilapidated and bleak after the com-forts of the hotel and of course I miss the glorious sunshine and the friendliness. We have not seen a soul since our return, although of course Lena is out at business all day so should have no complaints on that score and is often quite late back but gets quite waxy if I remonstrate. She will not allow me to do much in the kitchen, so if she is late I just have to go hungry! I should not mind this if there was some appreciation of my point of view but as you know that is something which is quite lacking in her makeup! Of course I have the wireless but it is not the same thing as Human companionship and I

45

think perhaps I have been spoilt by our talks during those happy weeks in Italy. However I do not mean to complain but I do not really think this arrangement can continue very long as the loneliness and bad temper is upsetting, and I wonder if you have given any more thought to Our Plan! and have had an opportunity of talking it over with Mrs Evans? As you know, I have some of my own furniture so could furnish the room if there is room but could of course put it in storage if that would be more convenient to Mrs Evans and bring just a few personal belongings, photos, etc. As to catering I do not eat a lot and Would be no trouble and should enjoy making a little snack for myself rather than give trouble if you and Mrs Evans wanted to go out. As to Finance! *as you know I am independent and am sure this could be arranged so that you would not be out of pocket in a perfectly businesslike arrangement and I do not thinly even Lena can complain on that score. I do feel I really cannot face the winter here with Lena out all day and quite wrapped up in herself at all times after the glimpse our happy holiday gave me of how different life used to be when my husband was alive. So should indeed be grateful to hear if you have had an opportunity of discussing it.*

I do hope you have had no further digestive trouble and that the pills were efficacious. How drab our English streets seem after the colourful—and sunny—*Italian scene!! Please remember me to Mrs Evans and believe me with kindest regards and hoping to have a line from you shortly,*

Yours very sincerely,

Cynthia M. Fingal.

Dear Mrs Evans,

Just to let you know we got back on Friday last after a hellish journey. We had nothing but rain after you left and actually took off during a thunderstorm, the Italians absolutely not caring whether the plane was struck or not. It was still raining when we got to London Airport but at least everything was properly run there, porters, luggage, etc., and it was nice to know which side the traffic was driving on and get some quiet! Not to mention being able to drink the water, tea, salad, etc. Hope your journey was OK.

I wonder if you have thought over what we discussed yet. Since getting back Auntie has been v. difficult and seems to think I ought to rush back from business every evening and listen to her woes! Needless to say it's imposs to even think of having friends in while she's like this or any life of my own as old people are so selfish. Of course she is fit and well as regards health, etc, and really no trouble to anyone with experience of old people, as you know, and its just unfortunate that she and I don't hit it off. If you did decide you could have her, she could easily afford 6 guins a week.

Could we meet in London one day and have a confab? I can organise a half day here if you let me know what date would suit. The sooner the better, as it would be best to get her moved before the cold weather starts.

Best wishes, and hoping to hear from you.

Yours v truly,

Lena Kemp.

EW ANMIE,
Greenlea Avenue,
Ellbrook, M'sex.

Dear Lena,

Sorry not to have replied to yours of the 27th before this but have had my hands full with getting things and garden straight after the holiday.

I have discussed your suggestion regarding your auntie with Mr Evans and we both think it would be possible for us to make a home for her here. She would have to be agreeable to this as we could not have any unpleasantness about her being moved and perhaps being unhappy to leave Reading, but that is up to you. I am sure we should both do our best to make her happy.

I shall be up in London on Thursday of next week when we could meet and discuss further. We could meet at the Civil Service Stores in the Strand as they are open till 7 on Thursdays and have a nice tearoom on the top floor. Let me know what time suits you and I will be there.

All the best,

Yours ever,
Maisie Evans.

3

'Happy the bride the sun shines on!'

'Oh!' Mrs Fingal coloured up like a girl as Josh helped her out of the hired car which, towards the end of August, brought her and various of her belongings to Greenlea Avenue. And the sun was shining, after many rainy days, so that the feature- less landscape which seemed merely an extension of the nearby airport, except that its concrete runways were edged with bun- galows and parked cars, was pearled with a humid warmth and the red, white and green of Ewanmie was as bright as the illustration to a fairy story. Instead of larks, aeroplanes squealed overhead. There was a smell of hot grass and petrol.

She stood trembling in the porch, clutching her handbag and a clock, while Josh went to help the driver and Lena unpack and carry in several suitcases, some pictures, a slender Victorian rocking-chair. Mrs Evans came up the path with a moleskin coat over her arm. 'It is a warm day, isn't it. I hope you got a nice breeze in the car.'

Oh yes—yes. He didn't drive too fast, because of the clock. What a great deal there seems! Yet I left my bureau. And the wardrobe Lena says I must sell. It's so big, you know, solid mahogany, cedar, no moths. . . . I do hope there's not too much. And in this heat. . . .'

'Don't you worry yourself. Everything'll be as right as rain. Let's go inside and see where to stow everything.clock.'

The chauffeur had dumped his burdens in the hall and Lena was pulling them through into the back bedroom. 'I'll do that, dear, you see to the man. Go and sit yourself down in the lounge for a minute, Mrs Fingal, while we sort ourselves out. I'll take the clock.'

'No, I'll keep it.' She hugged it to her but went obediently into the front room and sat down where she could see what was going on from the window, the clock on her lap. The chauffeur was shutting the boot, and Lena joined Josh, opening her purse. Josh spoke, Lena questioned sharply, Josh nodded, Lena turned to the man, who came round to them dusting his hands together. They all three talked, although Josh gazed down the street with an air of non-involvement.

Mrs Evans came into the room and looked out over Mrs Fingal's shoulder. 'Ah, they're finished now. I expect we'd all like some tea.'

'I hope Lena tips the man properly. He was most obliging.'

'Don't worry, dear, Josh will see to all that.' She tweaked the net curtain over the scene.

Denied, Mrs Fingal sat back. 'Men always know these things. Such a help. Porters and tradesmen, polite when a man tips them but the same sum from a woman, most extraordinary. Lena will haggle. I can't bear that. Meanness I cannot bear.'

'Josh will see him right. Now, let me take that clock.'

'No. No, thank you. I know its ways, just where it likes to stand.'

'Then let's go into your room and get it settled, shall we?' Her broad face smiled and with a hand under the elbow, she helped Mrs Fingal to her feet.

Apart from the luggage, set haphazard in the middle of the floor, the room was neat. Fresh curtains, a fresh rug before the electric fire, a fresh runner on the dressing-table, a vase of gladioli. The sun had left this side of the house but the prospect of lawn, garden shed and coal bunker was still bright with its glow.

'Now where arc you going to put it?' Mrs Fingal gazed

51

about, scarcely hearing her. 'On the mantelpiece? You could see it well there. Or on the dressing-table? Eh?'

'Oh, on the mantelshelf. It likes the warmth.' She manœuvred round the suitcases and set the clock carefully on the narrow shelf. She laid her car against the glass, knocking her hat askew, and nodded. 'It's going.'

'That's nice. There's nothing like a clock for company.'

'It was a wedding present, from my husband's firm. It's only ever stopped twice. But it loses a bit.'

'They do when they get old. Now you know where the toilet is, dear, don't you, from your visit last time. I'll just go and pop the kettle on and we'll all be glad of a cup of tea. Then when we've had that you can tell me which case the linen's in and I'll make up your bed. And I expect Lena'll be wanting to get away pretty soon after, weekend traffic and all.'

Lena stood in the doorway. 'I've sent him to have some tea, he'll be back in an hour. I suppose you want me to help you unpack?'

'We won't do much tonight, I think.' Mrs Evans smiled at them both. 'Just the linen and toilet things and a personal touch or two to make it seem homey, eh?' She moved towards the door. 'You make yourself comfy, dear, while Lena and I make the tea. I made a nice cake specially. . . .'

As they left the room Mrs Fingal heard Lena say, 'She can't digest currants . . .' before the door swung to behind them. She sat down on the bed, her hands clasped on her handbag, and stared about her; bounced a little to try the mattress; felt the pillow. Then she put her handbag aside, got up and trundled over to the dressing-table, removing her hat and putting it down on the runner embroidered with daisies and forget-me-nots. Her reflection in the mirror showed her bright-eyed, colour in her cheeks, her white hair squashed thin to the skull by the pressure of the hat. She smiled at herself gleefully, for to her it seemed she looked like a bride the sun shone on.

Mrs Evans produced a splendid tea, as good as that she had produced four weeks ago when Lena and Mrs Fingal had driven over to see the room and make final arrangements. Then it had been a sunless day and the electric fire had been welcome on the lounge hearth where now stood a vase of golden rod. There were paste sandwiches and wholemeal bread and butter, a jam and a chocolate sponge, both light as foam, all served on plastic doilies from a gilt tea trolly caparisoned in lace and linen. Admired, the teacloth was admitted to have been crocheted by Mrs Evans, as was (she undid the buttons of her cardigan to exhibit her massive bust) the jumper she was wearing. She had also embroidered all the cushions; and the table runner; and the footstool; yes, and of course the runner on Mrs Fingal's dressing-table. She was busy now on a set of table mats, their centres embroidered with a posy of flowers, their edges to be of crochet, an order from one of the needlework shops she supplied.

'She's worked up quite a nice little business. Keeps me in pin money, Mai does.'

She struck him playfully on the arm. 'Get away, Boy! It's just a hobby. I like to keep busy and after all, you can't be in the kitchen all the time, can you?'

Lena passed her cup for more tea. 'I wouldn't spend any. I haven't the patience. It beats me how anyone can enjoy slaving away in a kitchen all day.'

'Maisie enjoys it, don't you, Mai? Sometimes I tell her she enjoys it too much for my figure.' He patted his stomach gently, smiling at his wife, who smiled back deprecatingly.

'Oh well, good food keeps you cheerful.' She offered more cake, which both ladies accepted, Mrs Fingal with a defiant look towards her niece. Of course, when we're just on our own we just have simple things. But today's a special occasion.'

'You can say that again!'

'It's a new chapter for all of us. Isn't that so, Josh?'

'It certainly is.'

Afterwards Josh took Mrs Fingal for a little walk round the garden while Lena helped Mrs Evans wash up. Tea and a biscuit's all she's used to. She can't digest a lot, whatever she makes out. And she can't take coffee, it gives her palpitations. It took her weeks to get right after Italy, all that bitter black stuff she drank. She would do it.'

'Old people are wilful, poor old souls.'

'She'll be better with you, of course. I mean, she won't try it on like she does with me, always being awkward. But don't let her be a nuisance, with fancies and things.'

'I'm sure she won't be. Don't you worry about her.'

'Oh I won't, believe you me! I can hardly believe it's happened, meeting you accidentally like that and it all working out. I shan't know myself tomorrow, alone in the flat with no one to have to run round after.'

'That's the way. Just you relax and enjoy yourself for a change. You can start having your friends in now, can't you?'

'Yes.' She glanced at Mrs Evans but her back was turned.

'We'll get on famously, don't you worry. Just give her time to get her things round her and get used to the change. In fact, if I was you I wouldn't write to her too often to begin with, just a postcard every now and then till she's settled down. Of course you know you're always welcome at any time, but just to begin with . . .'

'No fear! It's such a journey too, all up to London and then the Green Line or the Tube. I'm not like Auntie, hiring cars.'

'It's a bit of a trek, I do agree, all the way from Reading.' She took off her apron. 'Now I'll just get her bed made up. I had to wait for her linen, you see, I thought she'd prefer her own.'

'It's in here.' They entered the bedroom and Lena opened the largest suitcase. It's her household stuff in here, sheets and blankets, winter clothes. And whatever she says, give her a draw-sheet, the rubber sheet's here. 'She handed the bedding to Mrs Evans, who was waiting by the stripped mattress.' Not that it often happens, mind you,' Lena added hurriedly, 'but better safe than sorry.'

Mrs Evans gave her comfortable laugh. 'Don't you worry, dear. I'm used to old people, I've worked with them all my life. Their little accidents don't upset me.'

'Well, they do me. I think it's disgusting. I think when old people get so they can't control themselves they ought to be put away.'

'What a thing to say!' Deftly she spread, tucked, folded.

'Well, I do. When they get so they can't look after themselves they'd be better off dead.'

'You're a bad girl, talking like that. It's a good thing no one else can hear you.'

Lena picked up the moleskin coat from the chair on which it had been dropped and hung it in the wardrobe. 'There's a lot of people would say the same if they weren't all hypocrites. Old people are just a nuisance.'

'It's a good thing we don't all think like that, dear. Josh and me are glad to give a helping hand. There, that's all nice and tidy.' She smoothed the coverlet back into place as the front door bell rang. 'That'll be the driver, I expect. How the time goes! I'll leave the unpacking till later and give her a hand when you've gone.'

They all straggled down the path to the car. Mrs Evans had given her some jars of home-made marmalade and a fruit cake and Lena put them inside with her coat before turning to say good-bye. She shook hands with Josh, giving one of her small, hostile tossings of the head as she drew her hand away, and then, warmly, with Mrs Evans. Then, after a brief hesitation, she bent and kissed Mrs Fingal.

'Good-bye, Auntie. Behave yourself, now.'

She got into the car, the door slammed, the engine started, they drove away. The Evanses waved, were silent, watching it out of sight; turned slowly, one on either side of Mrs Fingal.

'Well,' said Josh, 'exit Miss Muck.'

'You bad boy!' said Maisie, but she smiled; while Mrs Fingal laughed out loud, clutching his arm and giving it a delighted shake as she trundled between them up the path and back inside the house.

Packed in suitcases, Mrs Fingal's belongings did not seem much to show for nearly eighty years of living; but it took several days to get them sorted out. She insisted on unpacking everything at once, moving them from one place to another, dropping them, forgetting them, wanting them again, spinning from object to object on her bent old legs in a state of palpitating excitement, as though by displaying all her possessions at once she could assert conclusively her right to be here, making the spare bedroom of the Evans's bungalow her own, inalienable home.

As soon as Lena had gone she had started, binding Josh to her with appeals for decision and the steadying clutch of fingers. Where should the water-colour of her mother hang, painted when she was a girl, spaniel-like in looped hair and lace? And her books? There were not many but she must have them, and there were no shelves. The mantelpiece? Then where would the clock go, for it could not stand draughts and must have a surface absolutely firm? The photographs of her husband and her little daughter must be beside her bed, but the bedside table was small. And the photographs of her sister and brother-in-law, father and mother, every one of them dead but essential to confirm that she was alive, where could they go? And her clothes?

At this Mrs Evans put her foot down and got her to bed. We're not going to have you wearing yourself out as soon as you get here. A good night's sleep's what you need now and I'll bring your breakfast in bed in the morning.'

Mrs Fingal had not liked to say that she detested breakfast in bed, that she woke early and had to get up and move about to ease the stiffness from her bones and the melancholy from her thoughts—Lena had always complained that her sleep was disturbed by her aunt creeping and rattling in the kitchen soon after dawn. But when next morning had come Mrs Fingal was for once glad not to get up immediately, for the excitement of the previous day had tired her more than she expected, and besides, her thoughts were happy now. She lay listening to the recurring scream of the air liners rising or landing at the Airport, and to the beating of her heart, a tenacious but irregular drum. It was better to stay in bed for a while this morning, taken care of by cheerful Mrs Evans instead of scowled at by Lena. As she ate her breakfast, slopping a little tea on the tray-cloth and covering it guiltily with a plate, she could hear the Evanses talking and moving about as they started on their day. There were his footsteps going past to the front room, not stopping at her door; and hers, brisk, going in and out of the kitchen, bathroom, bedroom, a vacuum-cleaner's whine, a rattle of dustbin lids, taps running, his steps along the passage, a key in a lock, a plug pulled. Would he knock and come in to say good morning? The bedside table was too crowded with her belongings to take the tray which was weighing on her thin old thighs and distended old bladder, and somehow she had got egg on the sheet. It was her sheet, of course, CMF embroidered on the corner. She scraped the egg off but, alas, the knife had been used for marmalade. When Mrs Evans bustled in at last Mrs Fingal felt quite trembly.

By the time she was up and dressed it was nearly lunch-time; and after lunch Mrs Evans was firm on a rest—both of them always had forty winks, she said. Then it was tea, and a little walk to the corner, leaning on Josh's arm—the first time she

57

had really seen him properly that day; and after supper, television, and after the News, suggested bed, which she agreed because she did not want to inconvenience them in their access to the bathroom, although she preferred to sit up late.

Although this routine modified a little in the following days, it did not alter much. Breakfast in bed became the rule, as a convenience to Mrs Evans rather than a comfort to Mrs Fingal ('I can get on better in the house, dear, with you tucked up and out of the way,') as did the afternoon rest. So that it took a long time, split into many small segments, before Mrs Fingal had her room finally arranged.

Josh had hung her pictures for her: her mother on the wall facing the bed, the water-colours of Anne Hathaway's cottage and Holy Trinity Church on either side of the fireplace (she had been born in Stratford on Avon). She did not like to suggest that 'The Light of the World' should be taken down from above the mantelpiece, since presumably it hung there by the Evans's choice, but she avoided looking at it, letting her gaze rest instead on the six postcard-size reproductions of the Ravenna mosaics which she had bought in Rimini. The vase of gladioli was gone and had not been replaced; there was, of course, hardly room for flowers now all her belongings were unpacked, and besides she had twice knocked it over that first day, flooding the dressing-table and the rug. Her rocking-chair stood in the window.

Mrs Evans had helped her sort out her clothes, hanging those she needed in the wardrobe, folding the rest into the suitcases which Josh then took away into the boxroom with the others containing her linen. Into another they had packed all the things there really was not space for in the room—photograph albums, business papers, personal trinkets.

They'll be nice and safe here,' Mrs Evans had said, snapping shut the locks.

Josh had bent to pick it up. 'I'll put it with the others, eh?'

'Oh no—please, if you wouldn't mind.' She had darted forward, laying her knobbly hand on it, her head beginning to shake. 'I mean, they're such personal things, things I might really require at any moment, to verify, you know, or just to look at, not like clothes or the linen, which of course should go with the rest. But these, out of the way somewhere, on top of the wardrobe perhaps, or under the bed. . . . ?' She looked about, her fingers tight on the suitcase handle.

'It's a bit heavy for the wardrobe, isn't it, Josh?'

He hefted it gently. 'I think we could manage it.'

'If you could. They're just personal things, you see, that I like to have by me, papers and photographs, little knick-knacks I might want to have out from time to time, just to make a change.'

'Very well, dear, if that's what you want.' She had smiled Josh permission, and with a grunt he managed to heave the case on to the top, where it fitted nicely. 'But don't you go trying to get it down again by yourself without one of us here. You'd do yourself an injury.'

Oh yes, of course, I wouldn't be so silly. It takes a man for that sort of thing, I do remember, and things like fuses and getting taxis. . . . Thank you. Thank you very much.'

There it stayed, and when she lay in bed, during the long mornings between waking at first light (never accustomed to the shriek of aeroplanes) and Mrs Evans's permission to get up, she could look at it and know what it contained and toy with the idea of getting some of the contents out and putting some things that were out, away, well perhaps not just yet, next month perhaps, or at Christmas or in the New Year, to make a change. From the bed, too, she could look at the picture of her mother, whom she had never known like that, as a girl, but remembered only as the smiling thickset woman of the photograph on the dressing-table, and then only hazily, like an often re-read story, half dream, half true, for her mother had died younger than she was now.

Some of this she told Josh while he hung the picture, then when they sat together in what Mrs Evans called the lounge, or in the back garden, for the weather of that September was gentle. He would settle her in one of the canvas chairs with the newspaper and a magazine, but her babble of thanks would run on into a stream of talk and he would seat himself patiently beside her, turning to face the sun. Ah, it was just like Italy, Mrs Fingal would declare, the sun, the *dolce far niente*, niente, he and she sitting side by side as they so often had, did he remember in Rimini or Salvione or in Milan when it had been her husband, many years ago, of course, just after the Great War. Or it was not at all like Italy, depending on the coolness of the breeze which had rain in it, perhaps, making all her bones ache so that movement was a labour, although she did not tell him this. Sad thoughts came to her when her bones ached, although she concealed this too; thoughts all of the past, happiness taken away, loved ones who had died but who still peopled her head and her heart, so vigorous, so alive in her recollection that they forced themselves out of her mouth, a stream, a dream of what she had been when life was still happening to her. She tried to dress her memories gaily, for she was aware that even people as kind as Mr Evans were embarrassed by sadness; but the ghosts were sometimes too strong, and then her eyes would water, her head begin to shake, and she would touch his arm with her hand bearing the long-dead wedding band, and say, 'You must forgive me, such an imposition, all my troubles, but with you I feel I can speak . . .' With a little start he would turn his ruddy face to her and cover her hand with his. Of course, Mrs Fingal, of course.' She would clutch his hand for a moment, savouring its broad warmth, and after a moment go on talking.

If Mrs Evans were with them she was more silent. Mrs Evans brought with her a calm efficiency that called for discussion of the day's news or a knitting pattern or the television programmes. Mrs Fingal found herself always agreeing with what Mrs Evans said; and, glancing covertly at Mr Evans, she could see that he did too. If Mrs Evans were with them, after a little while conversation grew slow. Mrs Evans would knit, Mr Evans would pick up the newspaper or even close his eyes, and there was nothing for it but for Mrs Fingal to turn the pages of her magazine. Sometimes he would presently get up and go indoors. Mrs Fingal would long to follow him, but it was Mrs Evans who did. Mrs Fingal would remain alone, the magazine on her lap, in a garden where the wind seemed to have grown cool.

Every day, while the fine weather lasted, they took a little stroll along the pavements that led in one direction to the arterial road, in the other to the half-village where a few early Victorian cottages, some with shop-fronts added, survived among the glass and chromium chain stores, telephone kiosks brushed by old hedges, petrol pumps standing in an oily waste among the rambler roses. The place was like a derelict film set, bits and pieces of this style and that, and none of it worth anything. It did not even have a name. It was merely The Shops, or Sussex Road.

Near The Shops, even here and there on the nearby London Road roaring just out of sight, were one or two Victorian villas, reticent behind labour-making hedges, relics of what must once have been the village. There was even a late-Georgian house, now used, and meticulously preserved, as offices of the Borough Council. But the new roads which served no purpose but to lace one road to another, and all of them eventually to the arterial road, were edged with bungalows, each different from the other yet all without individuality, flat to the flat ground, centred in grass and lobelia, each with its television aerial. Their inhabitants were mostly middle-aged or old. There were no children.

The land that stretched around them was as featureless as themselves: fields of drab vegetables, sports grounds belonging to some nearby factory, a rubbish tip, a display ground for caravans, or just ground—stony, sparsely grassed, scattered with coltsfoot and shepherd's purse, bounded by slack wire. And beyond it, flatter than the sea, flatter certainly than the Sahara, the unseen, omnipresent, vast void of the airport

Along Greenlea Avenue, turn into Meadow Road, then left into Flowerfield Avenue, and you were at The Shops. It made a nice little trot for Mrs Fingal, clutching Josh's arm. Sometimes they went after tea, when Mrs Evans might accompany them; sometimes before lunch, if Josh had not already done such shopping as was needed and Mrs Fingal had got herself ready in time, a process which seemed to take longer each week. But they always went on Fridays, when Mrs Fingal drew her Retirement Pension from the sub-Post Office that lay behind the deep-freeze cabinet at the back of the self-service grocery store, Josh tactfully reading the notices about wireless licences and postage rates while Mrs Fingal counted the notes into her wallet. Then, if the weather were good, they might take a little walk round by the church—of no interest in itself but with some well-tended flowerbeds—leading back into Flowerfield Avenue and so home. There was really nowhere else to go except up to the London Road to watch the traffic stenching by, and there was no point in that.

The walk round by the church usually prompted Mrs Fingal's thoughts on religion. They were generally the same, following the lines of the first time they had come this way. She stopped at the gateway, ostensibly to admire the massed pinks and purples of the michaelmas daisies, but as much to get her breath, always a little short after prolonged movement. 'Such lovely colours, such a variety! When you remember what shabby things they used to be, no better than grey really. Of course, all plants need feeding. I remember my husband used to tell me what a great variety of plant life, and birds too, kinds you'd hardly have heard of, grow up on sewage farms. Not a nice thought, of course, but very natural.'

This cemetery's not been used for a good long time, 'remarked Mrs Evans,' I shouldn't think they get much of a congregation.'

'You're not church-goers?'

'Well no, not regular church-goers. We go Christmas and Easter sometimes, don't we, Josh, but I always say you can say your prayers wherever you are.'

'Yes. Yes. Quite right. Of course you're right.' She stood gripping the gate and staring over the grass bedsteads of nineteenth-century dead, meaningless now that everyone was boxed and burned, packaged and stacked in some necropolis. 'Although I sometimes wonder who one is saying them to. I mean, if He *is*, it just isn't possible, is it, every sparrow . . .? And if it were, then how could such terrible things be allowed to happen? So much that doesn't seem right, little children and all the concentration camps. . . . But of course, you're believers, aren't you. I remember Mr Evans telling me.' She glanced up at Josh craftily, reliving their confidences.

He inclined his head. 'I believe we're put on this earth for some purpose.'

'Ah yes, but what purpose? It's so inscrutable, one can't begin to understand—such beauty and happiness and all of it gone in the end, unless you believe in a life hereafter. One would so like to, meeting again just as one used to be, but I really never could subscribe to the Creed, not all of it, you know, I had to have mental reservations and of course that's no good. And they never really seem to understand Doubt.'

'We didn't much care for the Vicar here.' Mrs Evans began to move on and coquettishly Mrs Fingal attached herself to

Josh again. 'He was a bit too high for us and the people who went were all a bit too churchy. Once you get in with a churchy lot you can't call your soul your own. Join this, help with that, prying into everything—no thank you! I can't stand people popping in all the time, I respect privacy.'

Oh yes, yes indeed. No one ever comes to the house, do they. I mean neighbours, friends . . .'

'We know our neighbours to "say good morning" 'to, and that's enough,' Mrs Evans gave her a level look. 'Once you start getting too friendly you never know where it'll end.'

'Yes, of course. Yes indeed.' Diminished, she trundled on in silence for a moment. 'But Christmas is nice. One can enter into Christmas—the baby and the dear little animals. I like to go at Christmas.'

'I'd like to have seen one of those Italian services, eh, Mai? The incense and all the mumbo-jumbo. Going round with a coachload of tourists, you don't get the flavour.'

Mrs Evans chuckled. 'More like a railway station than churches, some of them. Or a Lyons Corner House before they went contemporary.'

'Oh, but the mosaics . . .' But Mrs Fingal shut her lips, glancing conspiratorially at Josh to share with him the remembered beauties. It kept her quiet almost all the way home.

Kingfisher Road,
Reading.

Dear Auntie,

Sorry not to have replied to yours before this but life has been pretty hectic. There have been a lot of juniors away sick (supposed to be!) and on top of that Miss Trent, who is head of the next section to me, got tonsilitis and was away over three weeks and of course yours truly had to pick up the pieces. Mr Bond relies on me, called me in last week and suggested I should take over some of Miss T's work permanently, he is very easy to work with so may do so, but it has meant wording late several days going over the files with him.

Glad to hear you are getting on okay with Mr and Mrs E, you are lucky to have found somewhere to take such good care of you, it sounds as if you are in clover. Mind you don't play them up or they will get fed up with you. Will write to Mrs E soon.

Must close now as have to go over some work with Mr Bond All the best,

Lena.

Ewanmie,
Greenlea Avenue,
Ellbrook.

Dear Lena,

Thanks for yours of the 15th. Glad to hear things are going well but don't overdo it!

Things are all right here and your auntie has settled in well. I keep her in bed a bit as she is apt to do too much and then of course we all pay for it. We had a little accident last week, I think she caught a chill and of course it went to her tummy, but no harm was done and as I tell her you have to expect that sort of thing when you are getting on. She is a dear old soul and gets on like a house on fire with my hubby!

Please do not worry about not visiting her, it is an awkward journey and not necessary as everything is going smoothly and it sounds as if you have enough on your plate at the moment!

With best wishes from us both,
Maisie.

4

With October winter began to close the windows and strip the flowerbeds. At first there were days of blue and gold but at night frost turned the dahlias black and then rain blew un-impeded across the steppes. 'It's treacherous weather,' said Mrs Evans, coming in for Mrs Fingal's breakfast tray, 'you'd better not go out, you'll only catch cold again.'

Mrs Fingal gazed at her. She looked smaller than she used to, for a shawl was round her shoulders over her dressing-gown and with her teeth in a tumbler on the dressing-table her face was shrunken in on itself. Mrs Evans had long ago given up making toast for her; bread and butter could be managed with the gums (although mastication had to be slow to avoid indigestion) and the more Mrs Fingal left her den-tures out, the bigger and more uncomfortable they seemed to be when she put them in again. Besides, she had had a series of ulcers in her mouth which had been very painful. Often lately she had been glad to be banished (pleasantly, of course, but without argument) into her own room, just to be able to take her teeth out. She could sit in her chair and rock; or if it were cold, she could get underneath the blankets—Mrs E. did not like her to switch the fire on needlessly.

'Not go out?' Oh, but I must go out.'

'What d'you have to go out for?' Oh, look what you've done, spilled egg on my nice clean traycloth!'

'Oh, surely not? I mean . . .'

'And on the sheet too. You are a mucky pup and no mistake. We'll have to give you a bib.'

'They're difficult to eat when they're not quite set. Eggs seem so unpredictable these days, they're all frozen, of course, and not the dear little hens one used to have running about in the old days.'

'I'll have to boil them longer then, won't I? I can't do clean sheets twice in the week.'

'Surely I brought plenty?'

'Yes, but it's the laundry.' She removed the tray and went to the door. 'You stay there for a bit longer, eh? No sense getting up on a day like this.'

'But I must go to the Post Office. It's my day.'

'It'll keep. You can draw it next week.'

'Oh no, I shouldn't like that I like to keep each week quite clear in my mind.'

'Well, Josh won't go with you this weather. His back's playing him up.'

'Oh, poor man! Has he tried a hot pad?'

'Keeping in the warm's what helps him. You won't get him out today.'

'Then I shall go alone.'

'You'll be sorry if you do, dear.' She went out and shut the door.

It took Mrs Fingal some time to do everything: to make up her mind to get out of bed and then actually to do so, for her joints got painful in the night. It was, of course, kind of Mrs E. to make her stay in bed; but at Lena's she used to get up as soon as she felt like it, with the whole day ahead of her full of small tasks, tidying, washing-up, little trips to the shops, even if she grumbled about them and certainly got no thanks. Here there was so little she had to do that it took twice as long to do it, and became twice as important.

With a guilty look towards the door, she switched on the

electric fire, and after warming herself a little began to put on her underclothes beneath the skirts of her capacious night-gown. Too late she remembered she ought to have washed her top this morning; as she dressed she had been looking at her Ravenna cards on the mantelshelf, recalling the airy emptiness of the church of which they were the only, absolute decoration, and repeating under her breath the exchanges she and Josh had later made about them. She really could not undress again now, it was too tiring and would take too long. She washed her face and hands and dabbed some cologne on her neck.

There was no one about when she cautiously opened her door, already wearing her coat and hat She was glad, for she did not want an argument with Mrs E., and she certainly was not going to make poor dear Josh feel that he ought to come with her, poor dear man. And she was quite determined to go.

It was a perfectly beastly day, with a mean wind blowing from every direction. It caught her as soon as she left the front gate, making her eyes run so much that every so often she had to stop and take out her handkerchief to wipe them. It was better in Meadow Road, but caught her again when she turned, reeling a little, into Flowerfield Avenue. She would have liked to sit down in the Post Office but there were no chairs. Her knees were trembling almost as much as her fingers as she put the notes away in her wallet, and certainly her signature on the pay-slip was most peculiar; obviously the clerks would accept any scrawl. At Reading the cashier would have looked at her curiously, even passed some kindly remark; but here, although she had come every Friday since August to draw her pension, the man did not even look at her. Slap slap slap went his stamp and the notes and the pension book back under the bars at her, with never a glance. There were two other old people waiting with her, and he did not look at them either. Nor did they look at each other, for like her they had enough to do to look after themselves.

By the time she got home she was exhausted. She was also late for lunch and had no key and Mrs E. opened the door to her with a frowning face.

'Where have you been? We've been really worried.'

'So sorry. It took much longer . . .' She stumbled and Mrs E. caught her and half carried her into the lounge, putting her in a chair. Her eyes were running and her limbs trembling, but worst of all was her heart, beating unevenly inside a cage that was much too tight for it.

'Sit there. My goodness, you've been a silly girl! Josh!' He answered from the kitchen. 'Bring a drop of brandy, will you. You had us really worried, going off without a word and in that nasty cold wind too.'

Thankfully she was aware that her coat and scarf were being loosened, her hands chafed and that Josh appeared with the brandy that Mrs E. made her sip. It went down like a globule of fire, igniting what it passed and sending its fumes almost immediately to her head.

'We'd best get you to bed. Can you stand up? Josh, give her a haul. Take his hand, dear. She's passed out by the looks of it.'

'Poor old soul.'

'Silly old soul, more like. You'll have to carry her.' With shut eyes, floating head and heart, she was lifted, after a good deal of grunting from Josh, and carried into her room. 'Put her on the bed—wait till I move the coverlet, her shoes'll be dirty. That's right.' With a thump she was laid down. 'I'll get a hot bottle. Take her hat and shoes off, will you, and she'd best have one of her pills, the brown ones. What on earth did she want to go and do a silly thing like that for?'

'It's her pension day.'

'I told her it could wait. Get her things off, I won't be a tick. All the lunch spoiling!'

Josh gingerly lifted her head and removed her hat, which had got pulled askew, then lifted each foot in turn and took off her shoes. He unbuttoned her cardigan, but paused at the blouse underneath it, then unhooked the band of the skirt, trying not to heave her about too much. When he straighened up again he found she was watching him, smiling.

'Trying to get you comfy. How do you feel?'

'Happy.'

'Happy? Well, that's good. That's first-rate.' He floundered under her smile. 'You had us worried, you know.'

'I do—apologise. Silly of me . . .'

'You need to take care of yourself, you know. Nasty cold wind. The wife's getting a bottle.'

'Such a nuisance . . .'

'You should have one of your pills.' He looked around for them but she waveringly caught his hand, clutching it with surprising strength.

'No need—it's quieter.' She carried his hand to her chest and pressed it there. He could feel the heart sluggishly heaving inside the bony skin and his fingers recoiled, longing for an instant for the moist rotundity of Francesca's buttock that day in Salvione. He gave Mrs Fingal's hand a squeeze.

'Just the same, you gave us a fright. You want anything like that, you just tell me, eh?'

She shut her eyes. 'You're so good.'

Mrs Evans bustled in. 'Feeling better, is she? Can you sit up, dear, I'll just pop the bottle in. Has she had her pill? Now I said give it her, didn't I? We don't want anything happening. Open your mouth, dear, and just let it dissolve. Well soon have you as right as rain. Go and finish your lunch, Josh, while I get her into bed.'

With another squeeze, he disengaged her fingers and left the room, exchanging with his wife a look mostly of complicity but just a little of shame.

Mrs Fingal was not as ill as she should have been, developing nothing worse than a cold. Nevertheless, Mrs Evans got the doctor, for, as she said as she brought him into the bedroom where she had kept Mrs Fingal in bed for the last three days, 'With old folk you can't be too careful.'

It was no easy matter to get Dr Preston to call, for he worked as strictly a nine-till-six day as a three-partnered Health Service practice enabled him. Most of his time was spent either at hospital or in Surgery. In hospital the work was so efficient and interesting, and Surgery so occupied with signing forms or letters referring patients to hospital, that you had to be un-questionably too ill to attend either one or the other before Dr Preston would agree to call. He knew Mrs Evans, however, having occasionally attended her previous old lady, and knew that as a trained nurse she did not call him in unnecessarily.

'We're feeling ever so much better now, doctor,' she said, tweaking the coverlet straight, 'but I always feel it pays to be sure, especially when we're newcomers and not quite as young as we used to be.'

'Quite. How old is she?' He snapped open the catches of his medical bag and whipped out a stethoscope.

'Seventy-eight—nine in January. We had a little tempera-ture for twenty-four hours—nothing much, 101.3—but we haven't one now. Just a little wheezy, you know, and as the heart isn't quite so strong as it might be, I thought it wise . . .'

'Quiet, please.' He sat on the edge of the bed, clapped the stethoscope into his ears and its nozzle between the buttons of Mrs Fingal's nightdress and gazed at the postcards of Ravenna. 'Right.' He disengaged his apparatus and stood up. 'Sit her up, will you?'

The examination, though thorough, was swift, and his Ford Zephyr vanished up the road within fifteen minutes, leaving behind him prescriptions for heart pills, sleeping pills and a linctus for the cough. He approved of Mrs Evans and Mrs Evans approved of him. Mrs Fingal told Josh, when he came to sit with her for a little that evening, that she would rather be dead than see the man again.

Even three days in bed had weakened Mrs Fingal's legs when Mrs E. let her get up again. 'It's only to be expected.' With a strong hand Mrs Evans supported her to a chair, 'At your age you've got no reserves.'

'But it's ridiculous, quite ridiculous.' Panting, she sat there, her hands clasped on the chair-arms, her eyes watering with anger and dismay. 'I've always been a walker. I used to walk miles. My husband and I used to have walking holidays, stay at an inn on Exmoor and tramp over the moors. When we were newly married. Dunkery Beacon, the Doone country—miles we used to tramp.'

'That was a long time ago, though.' Mrs Evans briskly made up the bed. 'We none of us get any younger.'

'But I must keep active. I've always been active. I used to tramp for miles with my husband, just bread and cheese and an apple . . .' She hauled herself to her feet and trembled the few paces to the dressing-table, where she clung. 'I shall soon get my strength back. I shall practise. I shall walk up and down.'

Mrs Evans regarded her calmly over the shaken, spread, smoothed coverlet. 'You do that, dear. But be careful you don't have a fall.'

After Mrs Evans had left she continued her crawling progress round the furniture, gnarled hands grasping, lips pursed or working silently, till at last she could stand clear and get across the room. And back again. And back again. And back once more, knees weak, a little giddy but mobile at last. 'There now, there now . . .' She had worn a blouse and a Harris tweed skirt and he had stuck a frond of fern in her hat and christened her Birnam Wood. Birnam Wood, she forgot why hit it had been a great joke then, and a splendid tea at a farmhouse with home-grown honeycomb and then the tramp home in the dusk and the smell of his pipe mixed with the wax of the candle beside the feather bed. . . . She was more than ready to sink into the rocking-chair at last, for the calves of her legs ached dreadfully and she had no breath.

Next day she not only walked up and down her room but presently stood near the front door, small and bowlegged like a Yorkshire terrier waiting to be taken for a run. 'I should like to go out for a little.'

Running the mop over the linoleum, Mrs Evans merely said, 'You can't do that, dear.'

'Just as far as the gate.'

'We've got too much to do this morning.'

'I could manage alone.'

'You're not up to it, dear.'

'This afternoon, perhaps?' She drooped, although her lips continued to form the phrases 'after lunch, after my rest, after tea. . . .' But after tea it was early dusk on rain clouds, and there was another day finished, like beads dropping off a string.

On Friday she was quite determined, putting on her hat and coat as soon as she had dressed and checking her big handbag several times to see that her pension book was in it, before going out of her room. Josh was in the lounge, dozing over the *Daily Mail*, She lowered her head as well as her voice, as though to be invisible as well as inaudible to Mrs Evans in the kitchen.

'Mr Evans—ssh—don't disturb yourself . . .'

'Eh? What?' He half heaved himself out of the chair.

'Don't get up, don't disturb yourself. Unless—I just wondered . . .'

'You're never going out?'

'Well, yes, as a matter of fact I am. Just to the Post Office.'

'Did Mai say you could?'

'Well, no. The subject didn't come up, there's no reason at all why it should.'

'I don't think you ought if she didn't say so.'

A flash of colour came into her face. 'I can please myself. Please remember I'm independent and can perfectly well decide for myself. Today is Friday.'

'It was Friday last week and look what happened.'

She came a step into the room, winningly. 'Well, yes, that's why I wondered. I *was* rather a silly girl, wasn't I, so I thought perhaps this time, if it wasn't to much to ask, you've always been so kind.'

'I don't think Mai would like it.'

'But you're always so kind. We understand each other, you understand I must get to the Post Office, but not by myself, I quite appreciate that after my little upset it would be silly, but with you I should be quite safe, if it wouldn't be too much trouble.'

He sat back in the chair, shaking his head. 'Mai wouldn't like it.'

'But it's for you to say. I mean, it's the husband, isn't it, and really I don't see why she should ever know. We could just slip out . . .'

He shook his head again. 'Better leave it.'

'But I can't leave it! It's Friday, don't you see?'

'Missing a week won't matter. It'll still be there next week, up to three months, I think it is.'

'You don't understand.' Her head and her hands began to tremble. 'I have to go to the Post Office on Friday otherwise my records will be wrong.'

'What records?'

'My Post Office records, of course! They won't be straight. Every Friday I have to go to the Post Office otherwise they get in a muddle. They can't keep track. It has to be every Friday.'

'They won't get in any muddle. You can draw it when you like, two weeks, three weeks, it just accumulates.'

'No, no! You don't understand . . .' She was shaking all

75

over now, her face blotched, and he got up and came towards her.

'Don't upset yourself. Here, you'd better sit down.' He put his hand under her elbow to lead her to a chair but she shrugged herself free.

'You've always been so understanding. I've always relied on you . . .'

'And so you can . . .'

'Ever since my husband died, because men understand business matters so much better than we do, and the little attentions I'm sure no one could possibly grudge. And they pay so much more attention at the Post Office if there's a man with you, apart from having your arm which she doesn't need like I do, so self-reliant and practical, it's the training of course. That's it, it's the training, an answer for everything but no understanding. But some of us aren't, you see, and you're always so good . . .' She broke off suddenly.

'Come and sit down.' He put her in a chair. She stared up at him.

'I have to go to the Post Office.'

'Next week.'

'Next week will be too late.' She began to cry, her face quivering under the quivering tears that ran down the runnels of her skin and caught in the hairs round her mouth.

'Here, here—don't upset yourself.' He patted her hands uneasily, then went to the door and called his wife. She came in an apron, a cloth in her hand.

'My word, what's all this about?' Josh told her.' 'Well, you arc a silly girl and no mistake. You couldn't go out in this weather anyhow, it's started to rain again. Come along now, take your things off and I'll make you a cup of Oxo.'

'She thinks she won't get her pension if she misses a week.'

'It's not like that, dear. It accumulates. You get a nice lump sum the longer you leave it.'

Mrs Fingal continued to cry, sinking down on herself as though the tears were draining her of substance.

'Or if it's really going to upset you, why don't you let me get it for you? You can sign the book authorising me and I'll draw it for you when I go to the shops. That's what we used to do with Auntie Flo, isn't it, Josh? We'd leave it a good few weeks and she'd sign the book and then we'd collect it for her. How would that be?'

Both the Evanses stood and looked at her. She sat like a small, crumbling stone under their scrutiny.

'Or Josh could do it.' Mrs Fingal's fingers moved on the handbag. 'That'd be best. You sign your pension book and give it to Josh and he'll bring you your money when he comes back from his constitutional. You'll do that, won't you, Josh?'

'Be glad to.'

'So you see, there's no need to get yourself in a state. You don't want to be thinking of going out with the weather nasty like this and you only just over your little upset, you'd only be laid up again. Now take off your hat and coat, dear, and go and have a little lie-down. Josh'll see to the Post Office for you, don't you worry. He likes taking care of you, don't you, Josh?'

'That's right, Mai, I do.'

'Give her a hand, then, while I make her that Oxo.'

Together they eased Mrs Fingal from the chair, and with Josh's arm about her, his fingers pressing gently under her armpit, she went back into her own room. She let him remove her hat and coat, let him lay her on the bed from which she had so recently got up, let him straighten out her legs and take off her shoes; let him cover her with the counterpane and arrange her head on the pillow, let him tidy her clothes away and give her a brown pill and put a tumbler of water ready in case she wanted her dentures out. She lay under his ministrations drowsily, and somewhere a response long moribund twitched faintly under his touch and his presence, while Mrs Evans, forgotten, made Oxo in the kitchen.

Maisie went up to London one day early in December, leaving a shepherd's pie in the oven for Josh and Mrs Fingal's lunch. Emerging at Marble Arch, she took a lift to the top floor at Sclfridges and worked her way downward, department by department. She did not buy very much: a pair of pyjamas for Josh, a box of soap for Mrs Fingal and, after a little thought, a scarf that felt like silk, with big pink roses on it, for Lena. She tried on a number of skirts but did not buy any of them; the salesgirl was driven to say that this was the best selection she was likely to find for a forty-two-inch hip, but Maisie replied sharply that there were plenty of other stores.

She lunched off a hamburger, orangeade and a peach melba, smoking two cigarettes afterwards, impervious to the crowds that by now surged and clustered for an empty seat. When she was ready she left without leaving a tip, for she was unlikely to be in this place again and even if she were, would certainly not have the same waitress.

By now Oxford Street was a lava-stream of people, clutched children, crushed parcels, the Christmas decorations bobbing above the traffic against a sky which was already growing dark. Solidly, not deflected, Maisie entered every store. In one she bought herself some wool-and-nylon vests, in another she found a skirt, at all of them she visited the needlework departments. She had saved the best till the last, the demure treasures of the Needlewoman, where she bought a good deal but acquired more by studying the pattern books and getting new ideas. She was ready for her tea and Lena.

Lena flung her nylon fur coat away from her behind before flouncing into the chair which Maisie had kept for her. She was late, her cheek and her nose pink with cold and hurry, her fine bust encased in a scarlet dress which matched an overcomplicated hat. She too had parcels and was loud with complaints about unsuccessful purchases, the cost of everything and the crowds.

'I just don't know why one does it year after year. It's only a commercial racket nowadays anyway. I'm sure I don't want people to give me things just because they feel they ought. And I mean, just think what the shopkeepers must make out of it, it makes you sick. Oh well, thank goodness it's only once a year. I'll have tea and buttered toast and jam and a bit of that gâteau.' She flung back her coat and self-consciously patted the hair under her hat brim.

'Well, how are you, dear?' asked Maisie, 'I must say you're looking bonny. That colour suits you.'

Lena preened a little. Of course my job keeps me on my toes. All the extra work and responsibility and the staff—you wouldn't believe what we have to put up with from some of the juniors, they have no idea of what's expected of them and as for hard work, they don't know the meaning of the word. As Mr Bond says, no one would have put up with that sort of thing when we started in business, you had to work then.'

'You're right there. When I did my training there was no forty-hour week and wage scale, I can tell you. Of course, that's years ago, before you were born or thought of.' She smiled, rearranging the tea things the waitress had brought.

'They've got too much money. I ask you, ten pounds a week for a copy typist, can't even do shorthand! No wonder the shops all encourage us on a spending spree.'

'Milk, dear?'

'Thanks.' She took the cup and stirred it vigorously. 'You look as though you've had a busy day too, all those parcels. Somebody's going to be lucky.'

'Oh well . . .' She glanced deprecatingly down at the bags piled on the floor between their chairs. 'I like to do it. As a matter of fact, there's a little something . . .' She reached

79

down and extricated the package for Lena, putting it beside her plate. 'For you, dear—just a thought.'

'Oh—you shouldn't have!' For a moment Lena looked quite angry, as though a gift were an insult.

'Don't open it now, it's only a trifle. But when it caught my eye I thought to myself, That's just Lena's style.'

'Well—thanks.' She picked it up and stuffed it into one of her own containers, then asked abruptly, 'How's Auntie?'

'Not too bad, considering.' She sipped her tea thoughtfully. 'Of course, she had a bit of a bad turn, you know, a few weeks back.'

'Did she?'

'Didn't she write you?'

'I've not had a letter for weeks.'

'Now I quite thought she'd have written you, she is a naughty girl! I didn't write myself because frankly I didn't want to worry you, and anyway we soon got her right again— we've ever such a good doctor, quite young but ever so good, on the Health, of course, but he's always got time for you, never mind how small a thing it is, nothing's too much trouble for him. Your auntie took ever such a fancy to him. They're not all like that, I can tell you. Some of the ones I've seen while I was still in nursing—well, it'd make your hair curl.'

'What did she have?'

'She was a very silly girl, really. She would go out when the weather was bad and although my hubby went with her, she overdid it, you see, and of course it went to her chest. It was touch-and-go with pneumonia, and of course with old people, and her heart not all it ought to be, that's the last thing we wanted. But thank goodness, it didn't get to that. With this young doctor, you see, and the nursing. . . . Of course, it pulled her down, I can't deny that. But she's such a game old soul, isn't she, you can't help but admire her spirit. Me and Josh have got ever so fond of her—and between you and me, she thinks the world of my Josh, it's quite a case! He takes her for little walks, posts her letters and so on—I did think she'd have written you.'

'To tell the truth, I haven't written to her. I don't know, the time goes so fast and I've had so much on my mind lately.'

'I'm sure you have, dear.'

'Since I got rid of Auntie the time seems to fly somehow. Of course, now I have time for myself without having her to see to all the time and there's always a hundred and one things to get done. Then there's a lot more to do with business, work to bring home in the evening and things to discuss with Mr Bond, we often have to stay late.' She glanced covertly at Maisie while scraping the last of the jam on to her toast.

'I'm sure he must appreciate you.'

'Oh well, men! You know what they are! If they can find a woman to do the donkey-work for them they're only too pleased. Of course, he's head of the Section and has a lot on his shoulders. They think a lot of him in the directors' room, at least old Mr Oliver does, the son's not so keen. He's jealous, if you ask me, afraid Mr Bond knows more about the business than he does, and of course he's dead right, he does. I mean, it stands to reason, he's been in the firm ever since after the war when old Mr Oliver started it up again on a proper footing, and he knows it inside out. It's him that's built it up, if you ask me. The son's only been in it a few years so naturally he can't know as much as Mr Bond does, and of course, it's resented.'

'It would be.'

'He never gets any help from the son and Mr Oliver's not always there, so of course he's grateful enough to have someone like me to talk things over with who understands the business. You know what men are, they have to have someone to bolster them up, give them ideas they can work on, and of course Mrs

Bond's only interested in the home and kiddies—although they're not kiddies now, the youngest boy's at grammar school. 'She cut vigorously through the gâteau, mashing cream and crumbs on to the fork. Of course, there's the other Section heads, but there's a lot of jealousy. He's been there longest, you see, and Mr Andrews, he's head of Accounts Section, he feels things ought to be done his way, he's got some hair-brained scheme for co-ordinating Accounts and Orders—that's Mr Bond's Section—under the one heading—his, needless to say —and of course Mr Bond won't agree. It's an absolutely mad scheme, anyone could see that, but Mr Andrews is so full of himself, so naturally he's not very friendly. Oh, there's a lot of spite and jealousy goes on, I can tell you, men arc much worse than women.'

'They always say, don't they, there's a woman behind every successful man.'

Lena gave her a suddenly cautious glance. 'Do they? I wouldn't know. I've never had much time for men, couldn't be bothered with them. I saw quite enough of them when I was in the ATS, thank you very much.'

'I'll never believe you were in the ATS! You couldn't hardly have been out of your cradle.'

'Well . . .' Again she preened a little. Out of the school-room. I went in the tail end of the war, 1944.'

'You must have been under age.'

'I was eighteen. I'm thirty-eight now.'

'You're never!'

'I am.'

'Well, I'd never have given you more than twenty-eight or nine. nine.'

'Oh, go on!'

'I give you my word.'

'Well . . .' Even her eyelids seemed to smile, lowered to-wards the rest of the cake crumbs. Of course, I won't say no one's been after me. After all, I was only a kid and you know what it's like in war-time. Men seem to think they've only to put a uniform on for all the girls to fall over themselves. I saw enough on some of those gun sites to last me a lifetime, I can tell you.'

'I'm sure you did.'

Of course, some of the chaps were quite decent. There was one—Eddie, his name was, in Transport—he didn't know the meaning of fear. The things he'd get up to! Crazy, a real daredevil. But most of them were just beasts where girls were concerned.'

'It's always the same in war-time.'

'Give them the chance, they're always the same. I mean, they're all after one thing, aren't they, even the best of them— that and bolstering up their ego.'

'Ah, it's natural.' Maisie smiled. 'They can't get along without us women. Mothers, wives or sweethearts—and I sometimes think it's the sweethearts they need the most.'

Lena glanced at her sharply but Maisie's face was bland. Only at the far back of her gaze did a spark lurk to kindle an answering spark far back in Lena. Lena's was quenched in an instant; she drew herself up, mouth prim, eyes hostile, fidgeting with the cutlery. Maisie swallowed the last mouthful of tea and continued smoothly, 'Well, dear, I must love you and leave you. You've got a train to catch and I must get back to my little family.' She looked around for the waitress.

'We haven't talked much about Auntie.'

'There's not much to say. You get on with your life and leave the worrying to me—when there is any.'

'D'you think I ought to come over?'

'Frankly, dear, I don't. It would only unsettle her. She's settled into our little home so well that I think it's really only kind to leave her to her own little ways and routines. You know what old folk are, they get used to things being just as they like them, just as they're used to. She's as happy as a sandboy with me and Josh knowing just what she likes, and anything coming in new from the outside might only upset her again.'

'But what about Christmas?'

'Honestly, I wouldn't make too much of it. Naturally me and Josh have been thinking about it, for we want to make it a happy time for the dear old soul. After all, you never know how many more there'll be, do you? I did just drop a word to her here and there, sounding her out without her realising, and she just didn't seem a bit keen on anything extra. It'd be such a long journey for you, too, wouldn't it, holiday trains and all. And in the end, perhaps not appreciated.'

'Heaven knows I don't *want* to drag all the way up if I don't have to. Holiday trains are always hell, and there's plenty I couid be doing over the Christmas holiday, I might have a few friends in from business or something like that. I just wondered whether I ought to come. After all, I've not seen her since she moved in.'

'And very wise too, dear. I'm sure that's been half the battle in her settling down so well. Old people are very sweet but they do sometimes like to make things awkward, don't they, like children they are sometimes.'

'How d'you mean?'

'Well, you know—little jealousies and so on. I think if you really feel you ought to come over and see her it might be better not to make it Christmas. I think she's got some idea in her head—it's just silliness, of course, she doesn't really believe it —about people only trying to get things out of her.'

'What people? Me?'

'You know how they talk. It's just making things up really, they don't really mean it. But once or twice she's said, "I suppose Lena'll be round at Christmas to see what she can get out of me"—silly things like that.'

Lena's checks suddenly matched her dress. 'I never got anything out of Auntie in my life! She paid for her keep, that's all, and I slaved hand and foot for her . . .'

'Of course, dear, I know. She doesn't mean it, she's only talking . . .'

'Two years I had her with me, tagging round after me all the time, even on holiday. I could never go oil on my own anywhere, get a chance to meet anyone . . .'

'You've nothing to reproach yourself with. You've done more than anyone could ever have expected, especially when you're not really related. I think you did wonders, dear, I really do. You don't want to think any more about it. You've got your own life to live.'

'And I'll certainly live it!'

'Good for you! Old people mustn't expect sacrifices from the young all the time. You think about yourself for a change and leave your auntie to Josh and me. She's perfectly happy, we understand her little ways and don't let them upset us. And we'll take good care of her now she's getting a little frail.'

'She's as strong as a horse.'

'Not now, dear. Her illness pulled her down. I'm not saying she hasn't got many years in front of her yet, but after all, there's no use blinking facts, and she's getting on for eighty. The doctor said she may go on for years but then again she might just snuff out like a candle. It strained her poor old heart, you see, any illness does that at her age—and she's so wilful too, you wouldn't believe!' She laughed indulgently, gathering up the bill which the waitress had tucked under the empty toast plate. Lena made a feeble gesture towards it. 'No, no, this is my treat.' She buttoned her coat and assembled her parcels.'

'I'll put down the tip, then.'

They got themselves together and moved to the cash desk. They used the Ladies' Room, found the escalator, went out into the gathering darkness through which rain was beginning to fall.

'Don't let that pretty hat get wet.'

'There's a 15 coming—I'll hop on to that.'

'I'll get in the Tube. Take care of yourself.'

'I will. And thanks for the tea and everything.'

'It's been lovely seeing you. And don't you worry about a thing, you just get on with your own affairs.'

'I will. Bye-bye.' She pressed away to the bus, jumping a little ahead of the queue.

'Bye-bye. Merry Christmas!' Maisie watched her aboard and the bus move off. Then, settling her packages more comfortably about her, she turned placidly for home.

When Mrs Fingal opened the small packet from Lena at tea-time on Christmas Day and found it to contain only a Christmas card and two not very pretty handkerchiefs, she began to cry. They were weak tears, ones she seemed to have used many times before, that knew how to swell themselves from the rheumy corners of her eyes and find their way slowly, in little fits and starts, down the familiar runnels of her face. At her mouth they paused, then groped their way through the whiskers to drop on to her chest.

It had been a difficult day, the climax to a difficult week. The imminence of Christmas had suddenly impinged on her and she had worked herself into a terrible state about presents. She had given up trying to go to The Shops herself; Mrs Evans was adamant in refusing to allow her out at all except, on the one or two mild days there had been, just to the end of the road and back with Josh. Even this she had found quite an effort—as Mrs Evans had told her over and over again she would. She had to cling heavily to Josh's arm and by the time they got back to the bungalow her legs were trembling and she was obediently ready to go and lie down and doze a little and listen to her heart and the Evans's desultory voices or the sound of television through the sitting-room wall. Sometimes when she half woke from her half-sleep she could not remember whether it was morning or evening. Only the voices next door and the fact that she still had her dress on helped her to get her bearings again; the dull, dark sky, sullenly lit over in the direction of the London Road, was the same at either time.

She spent a lot of time on her bed, under the coverlet. As Mrs Evans said, it was warmer than being up unless she were able to sit close to the electric fire in the sitting-room, which naturally she could not often do since it was, after all, the Evans's sitting-room and she was only allowed in it for an hour before lunch or on special occasions, of which there were, until now, none. It was understandable, of course. They were, after all, man and wife and did not want a third person with them all the time—although she was sure *he* would have welcomed her companionship. In the early days it had been different. When she first came to Ewanmie it had been summer, there was the garden to be out in, the longer evenings, the sweetness of no longer suffering Lena's bullying and blustering. Or perhaps it had not really been different, and she was confusing her memories with some other time—when she had first gone to live with her sister, for instance, the nice little house near Basingstoke where it had been summer for so much longer, or even Italy, the umbrellas on the beach like beds of ugly formal flowers, zinnias, geraniums, begonias, all bedded out in rows, and Josh sitting on the bench beside her in his thin summer clothes, listening so understandingly to all she had to say. She felt safe in bed, for there it did not really matter in which place she was or what the time of day, and unless she gave herself away somehow Mrs E. need not know she was in any confusion. Besides, there was no doubt about it, since her silly escapade and illness (which Mrs E. now told her had been much more serious than it had seemed at the time) she was not able to do as much. Her legs were definitely weaker; she was afraid of falling and, as Mrs E. said, perhaps breaking her hip; and if she lay quiet she could always now hear the slow engine of her heart.

How, then, to buy Christmas presents? Lena was easy, for when consulted Mrs E. had said, 'Money. After all, that's what she's most interested in, isn't it? Just pop a fiver in an envelope and she'll be satisfied.'

'Do you think so? Of course, she is mercenary, always going on at me about how much things cost, but at Christmas—a gift is so much more personal, something chosen, don't you think, even if not quite right, but personal . . . ?'

'Well, of course, she's your niece.'

'Only by marriage.'

'. . . and perhaps you know what she likes. But from my reading of her I'd say L.S.D. was the way to that young lady's heart. Then she can buy herself something fancy to try and catch a man.'

'Catch a man? Surely she's given up . . . ?'

'Don't you believe it, dear. With her build and at her age, that's all she ever thinks about.'

'She'll never get one. She's too wrapped up in herself. Hard. She'll never get one.'

Mrs Evans smiled. 'Why d'you think she was so keen to get you out of her way?'

'Oh no. Surely not. So hard and selfish, quite unfit for marriage . . .'

'Who said anything about marriage?'

'You mean . . . ?' Patches of colour came into her cheeks and neck, her head began to shake and her heart thump. 'How disgusting! That ugly, common girl . . .'

She was too upset to talk any more and Mrs Evans had to give her a sleeping-pill to quieten her down. By the next day she had forgotten the details but remembered the disapproval, so gave Josh three pounds to change into a postal order and seal it into a pretty Christmas card for her. But what reached Lena was only one.

A present for Mrs E. was comparatively easy; she had merely to consult Josh during one of their tête-à-têtes when he would come and sit beside her bed, sometimes chafing her hands if they were cold or even her legs if she had cramp. She did not know if his wife knew about this, which gave extra excitement to the touch of his fingers on her bones, stroking and pressing under cover of the blankets, bringing yielding warmth to nerves and knotted muscle, yet alert in case his wife came in. Josh said that Maisie would like a quilted dressing-gown and that he would buy it. And so he did, going in to London for it and showing it secretly to Mrs Fingal with the bill—eight and a half guineas, a handsome crimson-silk garment piped in pink.

What, she wondered, had he bought for her? Something as handsome but more womanly, something pretty, his own choice. Gleefully she held back the question she longed to ask, contenting herself with stroking his hand and giving it a squeeze, her eyes watering in complicity.

It was Josh himself who was the difficult one. She would not consult his wife. Her gift must be a special one, a private one, like their relationship. What could it be, how could she obtain it? Lips working, fingers fidgeting, she lay awake at night (or was it daytime?) worrying. Sometimes she thought of creeping out of the house and taking a taxi up to Derry & Toms, or asking the postman to have something sent to her on approval, or telegraphing Lena to come at once and make suggestions· But each plan had, she realised, something wrong with it. And then, quite suddenly, the answer came: Stanley's cufflinks. They were 18-carat gold, with a small sapphire in the centre of each. She had kept them always, with his tiepin, watch, cigar-case and cutter, evening studs, and tortoiseshell hair brushes, in boxes inside the suitcase on top of the wardrobe. It was difficult for her to get at them without help; and she was certainly not going to ask for that, for they would ask questions. She got up in the middle of one night (it really was night, quite dark outside and she could hear one or other of the Evanses snoring across the passage), put on her overcoat and slippers, pulled a chair over to the wardrobe quietly, quietly, and hauled herself up on it. Her heart was thumping like anything, with fright as much as exertion, and she clung to the top of the wardrobe for a few moments till the giddiness passed and she could get her breath. She was not tall enough to see into the case, but she fished about in it, fingers creeping, rejecting, feeling, recognising, and was able to find the links and clamber triumphantly to the floor again and take them into her bed and examine them there. She slept with them under her pillow and hid them in the box with her dentures during the day. She had forgotten to take off her overcoat and fallen asleep in it, and had to pretend she had felt cold in the night. She had also forgotten to move the chair from the wardrobe, but this she did not notice and Mrs Evans did not mention it.

It had really been quite an adventure. She had come to no harm from it either, which showed she was still active if she were allowed to be. She polished and fondled the links every night, memories of Stanley merging with expectations of Josh, wrapping them this way and that, tied with a piece of ribbon pulled from one of her vests. It was not very grand, but it was the thought that counted. She was impatient for the days before Christmas to pass, and hardly noticed there had been no word from Lena suggesting a visit.

Mrs Evans had put her to bed earlier than usual on Christmas Eve and she had lain listening to the laughter and music of their television, the tap-tap of Josh putting up the paper-chains, the children caterwauling one verse of 'King Wenceslas' at each front door and their brusque dismissal by Mrs E., the passing cars, occasional cheerful voices in the street, the sense of busyness going on beyond her closed door. She dozed and dreamed of presents, waking in the still darkness of early morning with yet more hours to wait. When they were children they had opened their presents in the interval between the return from church and lunch. She and Stanley had brought this forward to breakfast-time, for until her death they had always taken Christmas lunch with his mother. Breakfast presents had persisted for the ten Christmasses of Alice's little life, and after that the habit had remained, although some of the joy had dwindled. Here she did not know, and had not liked to ask. The big box for Mrs E., the small one for Josh, were on the chair where she could look at them. In imagination she could see his face when he saw the links, his fingers fastening them in—or perhaps he would ask her to do it for him—hear him thanking her in that kind, slow way of his. He might kiss her. . . . 'When Mrs E. brought in the breakfast tray Mrs Fingal was trembling already, eager to get up at once.' Merry Christmas, merry Christmas! The presents are over there.'

'Careful, dear, sit still. We won't think about presents till tea-time, I've got too much to do.'

The first tears of Christmas had fallen then, when Mrs Evans had gone.

The day had got worse and worse. Josh had gone off during the morning, ostensibly to church. Mrs Fingal had asked to go with him but of course it was too far for her. 'Could we not get a taxi? I should be so happy to pay, it could be my Christmas treat . . .'

'You'd never get a taxi on Christmas Day. Nobody's out.'

'We should have thought to order one earlier.' He smiled at her as he tied his scarf. 'We'll do that another time.' But that was no help now, and she cried a little more all by herself in the sitting-room under the paperchains, the plastic Christmas tree stiff in the corner under its garland of coloured lights, while Mrs Evans was busy in the kitchen. Josh came back rosy and genial and they all had a glass of port together before a lunch which was really excellent, for Mrs Evans was a splendid cook when she wished to be. Afterwards, although Mrs Fingal got obediently on to the bed for her rest, she did not stay there. She had a sudden panic that the links had got thrown away mixed up with their wrappings, and she had to undo the parcel to find out that they were there. Then she could not find the card that, went with them, and had to undo Mrs E.'s parcel and shake the dressing-gown out but without finding the card, for it was on the bedside table all the time. Then it was impossible to fold the dressing-gown neatly back again; she had to squash it in higgledy-piggledy and the lid would not fit on and the paper seemed now too small and she had lost the string. She was exhausted by the time Mrs Evans came for her and had to be reminded to put in her teeth (which had somehow got on top of her row of books).

There were not many presents for anyone, for the Evanses seemed to have no friends—a fact which Mrs Fingal had ceased to notice, for day had followed ordinary day in small activities and imposed routines. No more than half a dozen cards were ranged on top of the television set; but that was five more than Mrs Fingal had. Only the Vicar of the Reading church she had occasionally attended had remembered her. His card had the times of his Christmas services printed inside, but it was a kindly thought, sent to her at Lena's address and marked 'Please forward'. Her old friends had all died; she had lost touch with her sister's acquaintances after Peg's death and made no new ones with Lena. Lena—and of course the Evanses—were all she had now.

Which made the hurt of Lena's indifferent handkerchiefs so sharp. Two handkerchiefs, and not even good ones! Two Woolworth handkerchiefs and a sixpenny card, from her only relation after the three pounds she had been sent. The tears began to trickle down again and she could not be diverted by the bedsocks Mrs E. had knitted her or the box of soap from Josh. Like a child, she would not see beyond the demolished walls of her soap bubble which had encased her in its iridescence, promising scarves of brilliant colours, perfume, fine stockings, cosmetics, bracelets, rich warm cardigans, petticoats with frills and inset lace. Tablets of soap, bedsocks and two handkerchiefs were weapons piercing her with old age.

She could not even enjoy the Evans's appreciation of her gifts to them. She would hardly look, hardly listen, withdrawn into the cavern of her misery. Her days of planning and excitement had ended in rejection, of her and by her. She sat crying among the Evans's cheerfulness, the paperchains, the plastic tree, shrivelled and perverse, until Mrs Evans made her go and lie down; and then she wet the bed.

Christmas card depicting two Highland terriers looking at a filed Christmas stocking.

Inside:

Happy days, Gracie!

SEASON'S GREETINGS
and
BEST WISHES
from
J. Evans
When are you coming to visit us?!

Kingfisher Road,
Reading.

Dear Auntie,

Thank you for your Xmas card and P.O. enclosed. Sorry not to have seen you but no doubt you and the Evanses got on all right without me. After the Xmas rush, was glad of the rest and had a few friends in. Shall be too busy in the New Year to make the trek over but no doubt you will write me if you want anything. Best wishes to Mrs Evans.

Yours,

Lena.

Christmas card depicting a haloed star watched by the Three Shepherds, kneeling.

Inside:

I migliore auguri di
Buon Natale
e Felice Anno Nuovo

Best wishes for a good Year—Graziella. Please to pardon I not reply with much thanks for fotographias Kindly sent. They re-create kindly remembers of you and Signora Evans. Albergo Garibaldi is terminated the 15th Septembre and I work Rimini at shop sales. I think always of England. With sincere remembers.

5

Josh was in the boxroom, working on his scrapbooks. Filling a folding chair, he sat at the window looking out on sodden February snow, two piles of magazines on the table before him, a paraffin stove breathing warmth at his back. Amid the neatly packed lumber, which included a divan stacked with cardboard boxes, and various luggage of Mrs Fingal's, as well as a cabin trunk which had belonged to her predecessor, he fitted in like a nut in its shell.

Open but pushed to one side was the scrapbook for the Old Folk's Home. He made up two a year and gave a lot of thought to them, selecting pictures from Maisie's magazines when she had gutted them of their knitting and embroidery patterns. He liked to centre each page on one big picture—a flower arrangement in colour, perhaps, or some appealing child or animal—surrounding it with subsidiary illustrations on the same theme and supported by jokes and verses likely to comfort or cheer. Graziella's Christmas card would have made a good centrepiece but this he had drawing-pinned to the window-ledge, alongside the snapshot of her with Francesca, curling a bit now, and an even more dilapidated one of the ice-cream kiosk girl he used to joke with on the Costa Brava three—or was it four?— years ago; the holiday they had taken after old Miss Kenyon had finally passed on, before they had moved here and before they got poor old Auntie Flo. That had been a good holiday; he had been that much younger.

The scrapbook he was working on now was his own. He

worked on it only once a month on the afternoons when Maisie was making the rounds of the needlework shops whose orders she fulfilled. In between times it was hidden under the divan, right at the back behind a roll of matting.

The secrecy and planning involved in the maintenance of this scrapbook added to the spice. He would buy the suitable publications here and there, one at a time, from newsagents which did not know him, and smuggle them into the boxroom under his pullover and hide them under the divan till Maisie was safely off for the afternoon and he was able to get to work. Later there was the more difficult problem of disposing of the 'empties'. In the summer he burned them in the garden incinerator, but in winter he had to go for a walk before Maisie came back, or smuggle them out again one by one, and dump them on one of the rubbish tips.

Now he sat sucking a fruit-drop, whistling through his teeth. The boxroom was snug, old Cynthie in bed as usual, Maisie out, nothing to distract his warm thoughts from the 'lovely' round whose outlines he was meticulously snipping. He placed her face downward on the blotting-paper and sensuously brushed her with Gloy, then lifted her, sodden and malleable, and laid her flat on the page. With a clean handkerchief he stretched out her tits and her high black heels, smoothed and stroked her bubbles. She had a saucy look under her drooping lashes. He gave her a last, slow stroke.

As he waited for her to dry he turned back the pages and browsed a little. They were mostly 'lovelies', art studies, and one or two film actresses whose proportions overwhelmed their bodices. There was also a series of six naughty postcards he had bought from a newsagent in Soho some years ago; disappointing considering what he'd paid for them, being no more than nudes wearing lace stockings and, occasionally, an apron and feather duster, but pleasurable none the less. In a worn envelope, tucked into the back, were two postcards he had bought from a chap in the Pay Corps with him during the war. The chap had been overseas and got them in Alex. He'd flogged a couple of them to Josh for a couple of quid in order to take out a NAAFI girl and, as he put it, 'get it on the hoof'. These pictures really were hot stuff, too hot even to have out of their envelope. Indeed, Josh did not nowadays often feel equal to studying their gymnastic ecstasies, although he liked to know they were there. He would have liked to know a lot more were there; he would have liked to have travelled—Paris, Alex, Naples, places like that, where you could get really hot pictures. There was a whole house in Pompeii, this chap had told him, with dirty pictures painted on the walls; you tipped the guide and he showed them all to you, and if you tipped him enough he'd let you take a girl in too and show her, and that didn't half put lead in your pencil! He'd like to see that. He'd like to travel. He hadn't been able to find anything like that in Salvione; in any case, Maisie always kept the currency.

He turned a page and found a blonde hiding behind nothing but a huge straw hat, held like a wheel before her body. You could get hats like that in Salvione—and girls too, or at least in Rimini probably. He leaned back in the canvas chair, his eyes sleepy, having a little think . . . the girls in their bikinis, the sparking beach boys and the sexy shrieks, and Francesca with her love-bites and her moist buttocks. And Graziella, sweet little Gracie, with the little gold cross hanging down inside her dress, more like a child beside Francesca but sweet, the two of them standing there in the snapshot on the terrace of the Albergo Garibaldi. The next holiday they had he'd like to go back to Italy, somewhere further south, Naples perhaps. . . . It would depend what Maisie's plans were about old Cynthie.

The short afternoon was fading. He cut out and pasted in two more of his lovelies, and completed a new page of the Old

Folk's album, leaving it on the table for Maisie to see. He was on his knees, stretched to push his own scrapbook far under the divan, when the doorbell rang.

He froze, as though the eye of God were on him, then ponderously got to his feet. His impulse was not to be bothered; but if it rang again, the bell might wake the old lady and then she'd start calling him and he'd have to go in and perhaps she'd want him to rub her legs for her or would want to lie holding his hand like she so often did, poor old soul, and he just didn't want to be bothered with her this afternoon, with Maisie safely out and his thoughts so contentedly, satisfyingly, on his scrapbook.

So he went down the passage and opened the front door.

He gaped. He was speechless. She seemed tiny, standing below him on the path, smiling her curled sweet smile but with anxious eyes.

'Signor Evans. It is I—Graziella.'

'My dear child.' He moved, arms out, enveloped her hands in his, drew her in. 'My dear child!'

'Is all right? I should writ you but so sudden I am here . . .'

'My dear girl, my dear little Gracie, of course, of course! What a surprise—ssh, quick, come in the lounge . . .'

'My baggage . . .'

'Of course, of course.' He brought her suitcase in and closed the front door. 'Who'd have thought it—little Gracie!' He put his arm round her shoulders and led her into the living-room, bustling about to switch on the fire, draw the curtains, exclaiming, while she stood with her hands clasped, watching him with her smile and her anxious eyes. 'Well now, sit down, sit down . . . I can't get over it! How long—where . . . ? Sit down, get warm . . .'

She sat on the edge of a chair. The signora?'

'She's out, won't be back for an hour or two yet. Let's have a look at you—my word, little Gracie!'

He sat opposite, knees spread to accommodate his eager leaning forward. Neatly held together in her overcoat, neat shoes side by side, hands neat in her lap, she looked back at him.

'What a surprise, eh? I can't believe it. I was just thinking about you, too.'

'No!'

'I was, I give you my word. I was just looking at that picture of you and the other girl and thinking about you. And here you are!'

'You are not angry?'

'Do I look angry?'

She smiled without anxiety now. 'No. You look well.'

'And you? You're pale. You miss all that Italian sunshine—and the vino, eh?'

'Yes, I miss . . .'

'You'd like some tea. Or some coffee? I'll make some coffee.'

'Please, no trouble . . .'

'It's only that instant stuff, I'm afraid, not like at the old Garibaldi, eh?' He was on his feet but she reached out and laid a hand on his arm.

'Please do not trouble. In a moment perhaps . . .'

'Very well—let's have your news first.' He sat down again. 'Whoever'd have thought it, little Grade sitting there in my own armchair!'

'I am not sure how to find you. I take the train and then the bus. There is no telephone so I take a chance.'

'There's always one of us here. But I wouldn't have missed that ring at the bell and opening the door and finding you standing there. My word, I wouldn't!'

'I too am glad. glad.'

'How've you been, Gracie? How long have you been in England?'

She looked down at her hands. 'I have been six weeks.'

'All that time and you never let us know?'

'I am working very hard as au pair girl—in Westminster.'

'Get away! What, with some M. P. or something?'

'M.P.?'

'In Parliament—you know, government.'

'No, not that. Some business man, I think. Big house, wife, children—old children. Much work.'

'Decided the time had come to make that visit to Aylesbury, eh?'

The smile flashed. 'That I must do.'

'Well go together. We'll make a day of it. When the weather's a bit brighter we'll have a real day out, you and me, on your day off. They give you a day off?'

'Yes—no. Is that why I am here. The work is very hard, many hours, not good people. Today I go.'

'Go? Go where?'

'Go from them.' Colour swept up in her face as she glanced at him and then back at her hands.

'Well . . .' He sat back. 'That takes a bit of considering, doesn't it. I mean, giving up your job. Did they pay you?'

'I have money.'

'That's something, anyway. As long as you've got a bit behind you. It's easy enough to get another job somewhere, I suppose. You're always reading in the newspapers about au pair girls. The thing is to get fixed up quickly.'

'That is it. I am nowhere.'

'How d'you mean, nowhere?'

'Nowhere. That is why I am here.'

He gaped at her yet again, sitting back behind his belly with his hands on the chair arms. 'You mean you've got no lodgings?' The small gold rings in her ears glinted as she shook her head. 'But, my dear girl, you can't go wandering about London with no lodgings!'

'I not know where to find.'

'Anywhere—all over—some simple little hotel or a hostel

or something. There must be some church hostel or something . . .'

'But I not know where.'

'The wife'll know. Soon as she gets back she'll get you fixed up.'

'I cannot stay here?'

'Here?'

'Always you say "Come". . .'

'Yes, I know, but . . .'

'For little while only. Two—three days. I would work.'

'It's only a bungalow . . .'

'I could help the signora. I am good cook.'

'We haven't the room . . .'

'I could sleep on the floor . . .'

She had lost the alabaster look he remembered; her skin was sallow, with darkness under the eyes, and the delicate nose and chin, the curling mouth, seemed negative rather than fine-drawn. She looked fifteen or fifty. He said gently, 'You look washed out—really washed out. You've been doing too much.'

She shrugged. 'Too much—what is too much? If there is happiness there is not too much. But there is not happiness. Since Albergo Garibaldi life is not good for me. Everywhere in Salvione finish for winter. My mother find work in the fabrizio, they make the ceramics for tourists, no? My brother go to Milano, find work also, my sister is married. I go to Rimini to work in shop, big shop, few prices, very cheap, you know? Then I think I try England.'

'You speak English a treat now.'

'All summer at Salvione I speak and also in Rimini. I read always English books, and someone teaches me.'

'A young man, I shouldn't wonder.'

'No, a lady. I sew dresees for her. I would sew for signora Evans.'

102

'She sews for herself. It's what you might call her hobby.'

'Anything I would do. I am afraid to be alone with strangers.'

She was still sitting on the edge of the chair, coat still buttoned, hands still clasped, alert and anxious as a cat asking to come in from the rain. Another girl might have wept, but Graziella just sat there looking at him, pleading with every line of her body.

Behind his pink face his thoughts ground ponderously. 'Well now, this takes a bit of thinking about. We haven't the room, you see. It's only a small place, just three rooms—but there's the boxroom.' His voice sank away as his thoughts took shape. 'It's full of stuff but there's a bed. I don't see why not, just for a day or two. You could be quite cosy. Here, let's show you.'

He heaved himself up and she rose in a swift movement that seemed to light her eyes. He led her past Mrs Fingal's closed door and switched on the light in the boxroom. He had forgotten to turn the stove off and the room was warm. On the table lay the scrapbook for the Old Folks, scissors, paste, the pile of magazines. 'It's only small, but it might do you till you get fixed up.'

'E bellissima!'

'There's no basin or anything. We all have to use the one toilet, that's the next door—and you'd need curtains.'

'I undress in the dark.'

'You could be cosy in here . . .' At the edge of his thoughts he saw the room lit only by the stove, a dark warm den in which a girl with lace stockings and a feather duster lay exposed on top of the divan instead of hidden in an album under it; but he was too occupied with plans for Graziella to let the image linger. He pressed her thin shoulder. 'D'you think you could manage?'

'Ah si! E una camera molto sympatica.' She moved quickly

from under his hand into the room and saw the snapshots pinned to the window-sill. 'Ai, you have my picture I I and Francesca . . .' She bent to look, touching the curled print gently. 'Is like my home.'

'I was sitting in here, you see—I use it like it was a study, have my own things about me, out of the wife's way. This scrapbook, see . . .' He opened it. 'We send them to the old people.'

'Ah—so! You are kind.'

'No, no. It just gives me something to do.'

'No. You are kind. I know it.' She was serious, looking at him with a steady sweetness that disconcerted him. He began to lift the boxes oil the divan.

'We'd better get these shifted—and find some bedclothes.'

'Signora Evans . . . ?'

'No, no. Best get it all fixed up before she gets back.'

As he bent and stacked, slow beside Graziella's quickness, getting a little puffed, he became aware of cries, tentative at first but strengthening, from Mrs Fingal's room. Graziella paused. 'Someone is calling?'

'It's the old girl—old Mrs Fingal. You remember, the old lady who came to the Albergo once?'

'She lives here?'

'She's sort of a P.G.—paying guest, that is. The wife and me, we do our best for her. She's all alone, you see, so we took her to live with us.'

Graziella's gaze was tender. 'Is as I say—you arc kind.'

'Get away! It's just, we try to give her a helping hand.'

There was a note of panic in Mrs Fingal's voice now, so long unanswered.

'She is ill?'

'Well—frail, you could say. She spends most of her time in bed now.'

'Poverina! I go to her?'

'It's past her tcatimc—I never made you that coffee, did I?' He put his head out of the door. 'All right, Cynthie, keep your hair on. She gets impatient, you know what old folks are. Now I know where we've got some sheets . . .' On top of the late Auntie Flo's cabin trunk Mrs Fingal's two big suitcases were stacked. Josh opened one of them and took out some bed linen. 'There we are—just the job. We're a bit short on blankets, but the room's warm . . .'

When they had done and he had tidied away the paraphernalia on the table so that she could use it as a dressing-table, he went into the kitchen and put the kettle on. His movements were brisk, his step buoyant, he whistled. On the way to Mrs Fingal he paused to smooth his hair in the hall mirror, straighten his tie and bare his teeth to see how his smile would have looked to Gracie.

'All in the dark, eh?' He clicked the light on and moved genially across the room to draw the curtains.

'I've been so frightened.'

'Whatever of, you silly girl? You should have turned your lamp on.'

'I thought you'd gone.'

'Where would I have gone to? I wouldn't do a thing like that, now would I?'

'I couldn't find the lamp.'

'It's right here, on the table.' He came to the bed and saw the photographs on their faces, a tumbler of water spilt. He clicked his tongue. 'There now, you've knocked your things over.'

'I couldn't find the lamp.'

'Not much use your having a lamp if you knock everything over reaching for it, is there?' He got a towel and mopped up the water, wiped the photograph frames. 'Let's hope it's not marked the table.'

'Is it night-time?'

'No, it's not long gone five. I'll bring you your tea in a minute.'

'I thought I'd had my tea. When you didn't come, I thought it must be night but then I heard voices and I thought it was strangers . . .'

'You think a lot, don't you. Here, heave yourself up.' Roughly but jovially he put his hand under her armpits and hauled her higher in the bed, leaning her forward and plumped up her pillows, ignoring the collection of oddments she had hidden under them, and leaned her back again. 'You'd better smarten yourself up a bit, Cynthie. I've got a surprise for you.'

She shrank back. 'I don't like surprises.'

'This is a nice surprise.'

'Surprises are never nice.'

This one is. Look how cheerful it's made me. 'He smiled down, tweaking her bed-jacket over her mottled wrists.' Come on now, Cynthie. Buck up. You want to look nice for your visitor, don't you?'

She clutched the jacket. 'I won't see her!'

'Of course you'll see her.'

'I won't see her! Not if she begged me. Not if she were to thank me over and over again. She's common, no manners. Not our side of the family. She needn't think she has any claim on me now, after all this time . . .'

'What arc you on about?'

'She was always selfish, wrapped up in herself. Rude and selfish . . .'

'It's not Lena, you silly old juggins. It's someone a hundred times better than Lena.'

'It's not that doctor?'

'Of course not. I told you, it's a surprise. Here, get yourself decent.' He buttoned the jacket over her sagging chest 'Do you want to go?'

'No.' His fingers brushed her wattles as he fastened the top button. 'Brush my hair, Josh.'

'You can do that yourself.'

'I want you to do it.'

'Well, only just to smarten you up for your visitor.' He fetched the hairbrush and she bent her head forward so that he could smooth the thin hair through which the skull showed. 'There now.'

'Will I do?'

'Just about.'

'Give me my kiss, then. You haven't given me my kiss.'

'Haven't given you your tea, either.' He went to the door. 'You lay there a minute and be a good girl.' She lay without moving, staring at the door.

Graziella had taken off her coat. She wore a black sweater from which her neck rose delicate and colourless. She came forward, Josh beaming behind her, and took Mrs Fingal's hand.

'Buona sera, signora.'

'It's Gracie—young Graziella from Salvionc, remember? We used to have some fine conversations, didn't we, in the old Albergo? Now here she is turned up in London, give us a good old surprise.'

'You arc not well, signora?'

'Of course she's well—she's just not as young as she was, eh? Say how-d'ye-do to Gracie, now. She's surprised, that's what it is. We don't have many visitors and it's taken her by surprise. Cat got your tongue, Cynthie?'

'I want my tea.'

'I do it, signora.'

'No, no, Josh must do it. I don't want her to do it.'

'She gets ideas, you know. All right, old girl, I'll get your tea. I won't be a tick.'

Graziella stood quietly by the bed, letting Mrs Fingal

examine her. For several minutes there was silence, save for the ticking of the clock and the wheeze of Mrs Fingal's breathing and outside Josh whistling in the kitchen and moving crockery about.

'Where did he say you were from?'

'Salvionc, signora—Italia.'

'Not Milan?'

'No, signora.'

'I was in Milan many years ago—after the Great War. With my husband. We spent several weeks there, on business. We used to sit by the sea and cat ices.'

'Not the sea, signora, Salvione has the sea.'

'Has it? We used to sit by the sea and talk about the mosaics. Such pretty mosaics, little lambs and flowers and birds, quite lovely. We always agreed they were quite lovely.'

'I know them, signora. They are beautiful.'

'You do? You know them? You must have been to Milan, then. Of course, it's years ago now, soon after the Great War, but I'll never forget them. I have postcards of them, on the mantelshelf . . .' She leaned forward to point and Graziella went to them. They were curled now and dust came off on her fingers.

'Ah si, these I know—the little sheep and the Empress with her ladies. And Our Lord in the green field.'

'Yes, yes, and the doves. All little pieces of stone, you know, no bigger than postage stamps—think of it!—put together to make such beautiful pictures.'

'In Salvione are still made the mosaics. Not so beautiful now, for the turismo. And much ceramiche, dishes, pictures, all.'

'What did he say your name was?'

'Graziella. Graziella Torroni. I am from Salvione, near Rimini.'

'I've been to Rimini. I met Mr Evans there.'

'I too. I work in the hotel.'

'What hotel?'

'In Salvione.'

'Why are you here then?'

'To work.'

They regarded one another for a moment. Then the old lady leaned forward, hunching the shabby bedjacket to her neck, her gaze darting to the door, her voice a whisper. 'You'll get no change out of her. No indeed. I'd go somewhere else if I were you. She's hard. Very hard. She was a nurse, you know —bossy. He's loyal, of course, never complains. But I can tell. He's sensitive, it must be a disappointment to him. I'd go somewhere else if I were you. Ssh!' She sank back, pulling the bedclothes up to her chin defensively at the rattle of crockery outside, but relaxed when she saw it was Josh.

'Here we are then. Here's yours, Cynthie—mind you don't spill it this time.' He set the poured cup down on the bedside table. 'Gracie and me'll take ours into the lounge.'

Mrs Fingal struggled up, her eyes on a plate of sandwiches which remained on the tray. Graziella helped her to sit comfortably, and put the teacup into her gnarled hands.

'You've made sandwiches.'

'I reckon Grade must be peckish.'

'Signora?'

'Don't give her one, Gracie. They're cheese, they'll give her bellyache.'

'I didn't have any lunch.'

Of course you had lunch! Mai gave it to you before she went off. You'll forget your own name next!' He rolled his eyes at Graziella.

'I should like a sandwich.'

'Well . . .' Graziella was looking at him. 'All right, then— but you'll pay for it, you know, and don't blame me.'

Eagerly Mrs Fingal took a sandwich, hesitating a moment

109

to find the largest. The tea slopped into the saucer and Graziella took it from her and put it on the table.

'You'll get in a proper mess, you will. Let's leave her to it, Gracie.'

'Should we not stay?'

'She's best alone. And it's more cosy in the lounge.'

'Let us stay just for the tea.'

'Well—very well then, just this once. We'd best have the fire on, then.' He set down the tray and switched on the one-bar electric fire. Graziella drew up the two cane chairs to the side of the bed and sat down. She smiled on both old people. 'Ecco! Now we arc good.'

Josh delayed longer than usual that evening before joining his wife in their bedroom. He had managed to avoid being alone with her since her return at supper-time, or even to acknowledge that there might be any cause for displeasure. Blandly he had retreated behind Graziella's presence; the brusqueness of Mai's responses, the coldness of her stare he had been able to ignore. But now she waited for him. He checked the catches on the windows, the front and back door locks, the switches of fire and television; straightened rugs, shook up cushions, went along the passage. There were no further tasks. The unaccustomed line of light under the door of the boxroom gave him pleasure. He could imagine Gracie moving within the small space, and paused for a moment listening for sounds, the rustle of garments being discarded, the creak perhaps of a bedspring. There was only silence. Reluctantly, he moved on.

Maisie was already undressed and stood clipping her grey curls into Kirbigrips in front of the mirror. In the quilted dressing-gown which had been Mrs Fingal's Christmas present to her, her back was massive. She said nothing. Josh moved lightly to his side of the room and, whistling through his teeth, began to take off his clothes. Warily keeping his attention on his wife, he allowed his imagination to flit through the lath and plaster to the boxroom.

He had got his pyjama jacket on and had modestly turned to the wall to remove his trousers before Maisie spoke. 'I'm waiting to hear what your idea is.'

'Mm? What?'

'Your idea.'

'Idea?' Glancing over his shoulder he saw only her reflection staring at him from the mirror, her quilted back, her hands clipping the curls.

'You must have some idea. Even you couldn't be so daft as to just invite the girl to stay.'

'Oh, you mean Gracie. Yes. My word, it was a surprise to find her on the doorstep!'

'You didn't by any chance invite her?'

'Me? Come off it, Mai. I wouldn't do that.'

Her implacable gaze accepted the truth of this. 'What's she here for then?'

'Well now, Mai—we couldn't let her go off again with no place to go, now could we? Poor little kid, no place to go, not speaking the lingo . . .'

'There's nothing wrong with her English.'

'No, she's picked it up quick, hasn't she? She's a bright kid, I spotted that in Italy. Fancy her latching on to us like that, remembering our address and that. Touching, really.'

Maisie turned from the mirror and, twitching the dressing-gown to one side, got into bed. Sitting up against the pillows, hands folded on her stomach, she gave the impression of being still fully clothed. 'I'm waiting to hear what your idea is.'

'Idea? Well, I don't know that I'd say an idea . . .' He slipped his long pants off his behind and sat down quickly on the bed with his back to her to peel them from his legs and slip on and up the pyjama trousers.

Her voice was calm. 'She's not staying here, I can tell you that.'

'Well now, Mai . . .'

'Tomorrow, or the latest Saturday, she's out.'

'Now wait a minute, Mai, the poor kid. . .'

'There's plenty of places she can go—YWCA, hostels—I suppose she's a Roman? The priests can find her a place.'

'It's not so easy, as quick as that. I mean, she's had a rough time, coming over here out of the blue and landing up with no better than slave-drivers. It's been a bad experience for her.'

'You've only her word for it. You'd fall for any tale these girls will tell you.'

'Now, Mai, that's not fair.' He gazed at her reproachfully, knotting the pyjama cord round his belly. 'She's a nice kid, you saw that yourself in Italy, always a smile and not with her hand out like a lot of them.'

'She's not staying here.'

'Just till she gets her bearings . . .'

Maisie's hands and lips tightened. When she spoke her voice was colder than ever. 'I sometimes wonder how you get by. You've got a cloth head, Boy, you really have. I sometimes think that old Grannie of yours must have kept you retarded. You'd have been better off in an orphanage, seems to me, rather than staying on that old girl's apron-strings. At least you'd have had to learn to think in an orphanage, more than beyond the end of your nose.' He turned away sulkily and began winding his watch as her sharp voice continued quietly. 'Use your loaf, Boy. Have a try, go on. Don't leave it all to me. What's she going to make of old Cynthie, eh? D'you really think we want someone else here now?'

'I don't know what you mean.'

'Yes, you do. You're not as thick as all that And don't think I am, either. I can read you like a book.'

His face had grown pinker than usual and he turned further

away, folding his trousers, hanging his jacket over the back of a chair. After a moment he said, 'I thought she might be just what we needed.'

'How?'

'Someone in the house. A stranger, independent. She needn't stay long, a few weeks. People could see we had nothing to hide.'

The grey ice of Maisie's eyes seemed to shift and form into different patterns. She said nothing.

'After all, no one else saw poor old Auntie Flo. I mean, we never had any visitors, witnesses, only the doctor a couple of times. That worked out okay the once, but when Gracie turned up I thought, Hullo, maybe here's a good thing. I mean, we don't have visitors now, do we, and you never know, when it comes to it people might think things. It might look funny if we turned the girl away, as if we had something to hide.'

'Who would know?'

'Well, like you said, she's a Roman Catholic. I don't know, there's priests and things, confession. She'd have to go somewhere, wouldn't she, it might sound funny if she said we turned her out in a hurry. But if we let her stay for a bit, it's all open and above board. If anyone asked, she could say how well we looked after the old girl. And it's not as if she was English. I mean, she wouldn't know about pensions and things, wouldn't ask questions. She could take some of the work off you, too, cooking and that.'

A faint sun began to gleam on the ice. 'And leave me more free for the nursing.'

'That's right. She needn't have anything to do with Cynthie bar taking her meals and so on, perhaps along the passage. But she'd be an outside observer, if it ever came in question. You never know.'

The sun came right out. 'Joshie my boy, you may be right. I do believe you may be right. Just for a week or two until she finds herself a job. We'll give her her board and she can do the washing-up and go to the shops—get Cynthie's prescriptions too, that'd be a good move. You're a good boy, Joshie.'

She beamed on him, and blushingly he approached the bed, turned back the covers and got in beside her. She divested herself of the dressing-gown, gave his ear a tweak, and lay down. He turned off the light.

'But mind now, it's not for long. When I say she's to go, she goes.'

'That's right, Mai. Always has been.'

'That's my boy.' She chuckled, turned on her side with her back to him and was silent.

Josh too turned on his side away from her, one hand tucked up under his neck, the other between his thighs. Back to back they lay, half-smiling in the labrynth of their drowsy thoughts, hers cold as clockwork, his warm and simple as those of a schoolboy.

Next morning Mrs Evans was all sweetness and light; and during the day Graziella quickly learned how to please her. In the afternoon they went to The Shops, where Mrs Evans explained things in each of those she dealt with regularly in a way which made it plain to the assistants that the girl was part of her household. Josh remained at home but took advantage of their absence to examine all Graziella's belongings, of which there were few, and to slide his scrapbook under the carpet under the divan for extra safety.

Graziella did all the washing-up and carried the trays in and out for Mrs Fingal; and Mrs Evans agreed to her bringing them cups of tea in bed before she herself rose to prepare the breakfast. She was awake next morning when Graziella brought them in, sitting up neat and buttoned, as though she could never be taken unaware; but Josh was asleep and reared up, his face pinker than ever, clutching the pyjama jacket close to his throat, smoothing his silvery hair. 'Mm—what? Oh—Gracie. Thank you, Gracie—grazie, very kind. Buon giorno, eh, Gracie?'

'Prego.' Smiling, seeming not to look at either of them as she had learned at the Albergo Garibaldi, she set down the tray and left. In five minutes' time Mrs Evans would get up, go to the bathroom and then come into the kitchen fully dressed, as though it were still yesterday, to cook the breakfast. He would rise after his wife, take longer in the bathroom, eat his breakfast in trousers, vest and dressing-gown, the stubble frosty on his pink jowls.

When Graziella left their bedroom she poured another cup for Mrs Fingal. The old lady by on her back, her mouth a little open and sunken in over her gums. Blanched and small on the pillow, her head looked like that of a ventriloquist's dummy. She started awake as Graziella set down the saucer.

'Who is it? Who are you? Go away,' shrinking down under the bedclothes.

'It is I, Graziella.'

'What do you want? I haven't got anything.'

'I have brought tea. You like tea?'

Her gasping slowed a little. 'Who are you? You're not Lena.'

'I am Graziella. You remember, I arrive two days past?'

'Where's Josh? Does Josh know?'

'Si, si, signor Josh is in his bed, drinking the tea as you do. Come, I help.' Warily Mrs Fingal allowed herself to be sat up against the pillow, her bed-jacket put on and buttoned. She smelled stale. 'Drink while is hot.'

She took the cup and saucer, holding them close under her chin. 'You don't live here.'

'For a little while I live. And you?'

'Oh yes, I live here. Certainly I live here. I'm a paying guest. I have every right to be here.' She refused to say any more, watching suspiciously until Graziella left the room, waiting for Mrs Evans to bring her breakfast and for Josh, fed, shaved, emptied, jovial, to look in on her, chaff her a little, brush her hair perhaps, perhaps even give her a kiss.

After breakfast Mrs Evans ran the hall over with a mop and the lounge with the Hoover before going in to Mrs Fingal to get her up, help her wash and dress, and sit her in the rocking-chair, which had been moved into the lounge. She could look out of the window and watch for Josh to come back from his walk or talk to him if he were in, while Mrs Evans cooked the lunch. Afterwards she was undressed and put back to bed again. Everyone rested, Josh in the lounge asleep in the arm-chair, until tea-time, so there was no point in keeping her up. Sometimes Mrs Evans went shopping, a fourpenny bus ride along the London Road to the nearest centre, to buy silks or wools or delicacies she and Josh liked which The Shops did not stock. It made, as she said, a break. After tea came tele-vision, which Mrs Fingal could hear through the wall, and supper to prepare and eat, Mrs Fingal to settle for the night, more television, a hot drink, bed. It was a full day.

Into it Graziella was at pains to fit as neatly as a piece of jigsaw puzzle. She quickly perceived which chores Mrs Evans was willing to relinquish and which she would retain. She retained absolute control of the old lady, allowing Graziella only to waken her in the mornings, open the curtains, sit her up and draw her gently into the new day, to carry her trays, empty her slops. Mrs Evans wished to do all the cooking but Graziella could wash up, prepare vegetables, wash the floors and clean the oven. She could also do the washing, which Josh had hitherto taken once a week to the launderette, and which often involved Mrs Fingal's bed linen.

Graziella did it all smilingly. She had washed sheets often enough in Salvione, pegging them out in lines on the Albergo's rooftop to catch the brilliant air in their sails, or run out on pulleys across the narrow lane beside her home. She would have liked to cook, but appreciated that the provision of meals was the privilege of the head woman of the household. She was quick to offend in nothing, to placate in everything, withdrawing to the boxroom when her work was done rather than risk Mrs Evans's possible resentment at Josh's gallantries. Often she went out in the afternoons when they rested, quartering the wastelands of Meadow Road and Flowerfield Avenue, The Shops, the London Road. The landscape was not dissimilar to that round Salvione: flat, characterless, the fields half-cultivated, half-industrialised, the proliferation of expedient building, and the arterial road with its whipping, stenching traffic. But beyond it there was not the sea, placidly lipping the sand and the little crabs; and beyond cabbage fields and concrete factories were not the mountains, over whose spine lay patrician cities. For all Graziella knew, this wasteland extended indefinitely, was all England. And over it was a sky pierced by aircraft, that was never the same from one hour to the next unless to be a sullen grey, that never surrendered itself to being bountiful. In Salvione the rain poured itself out of purple clouds extravagantly, like a Verdi opera. Here it stung from a closed sky, spitefully. The houses and factories seemed closed too, as though people did not use them. Even the disarray was neat, without profusion. Only the flowers gave—swathes of crocuses in the prim bungalow gardens and the shimmer of forsythia.

Graziella walked along the well-kept pavements, free from puddles, with their concrete kerbs which did not crumble, looking at the shops, which were better arranged, certainly better lit than those at home, and at the people whose natures she could not guess behind their non-committal faces. To her it seemed they smiled but never laughed, disapproved but never grew angry. Apart from occasional squawking youths, no one ever spoke loudly. There was no sound but the aeroplanes and the traffic, or in the quieter roads one's own footfalls and, increasingly as the days passed, the birds, concealed in the small trees but swelling with springtime, even here.

Returning, she let herself quietly in through the back door, for she did not want to disturb Mrs Evans or bring Josh out to her. Her room was cool, for she did not like to burn the paraffin stove too much. She removed her coat and scarf and lay down on the bed, her rough, long-fingered hand over her stomach. For a while she dozed; when she got up again she knelt by the bedside, resting her forehead on the hands through which the rosary passed, bead by bead. She tried not to weep; but it was difficult.

In so small a house it was necessary for each person to move with wariness if their private purposes were to be protected from discovery. In the kitchen, in and out the other rooms, Mrs Evans moved placidly, secure in ownership. In the living-room Josh lurked, waiting behind his paunch, his bland blue eyes, his newspaper. In the boxroom Graziella hid, perched among the bric-à-brac like a transient bird, nothing of her own to show but a few clothes, a crucifix, a picture of a Raphael madonna and of her mother. Once, the week after Graziella had arrived, when Mrs Evans had gone to the Post Office, Josh had knocked on the door with a request for his Old Folk's scrapbook. He had been slow finding it and there was not much space for two people in the small room, which had led to a good deal of jocular contact. Smilingly Graziella had excused herself and gone in to Mrs Fingal, who, like the other two, both hid and waited, feverishly watching for Josh to visit her or dozing against her pillows. She awoke to see Graziella sitting in the dusk by the bedside. 'Who's that? Is it Alice?'

'It is Graziella.'

'Graziella. I thought you were Alice. Of course not, how silly of me. But just for a moment . . .'

'Who is Alice, signora?'

'No one. Of course not. She was only a child. How old arc you?'

'Twenty years, signora.'

'That's what I thought. Of course not. Besides, you're dark.'

'In Italia are many dark people.'

'Naturally. They're Latins. Latins arc always dark. Alice was fair.'

'She was of your family?'

'She was only ten—such a bright, pretty child. Peritonitis, it was—they didn't realise, you see. She was ten.'

'Ai, to lose a child! God will not forget.'

'God? You're a Papist, I suppose.'

'Si, signora.' Graziella rose, switched on the lamp and went to draw the curtains. The old lady watched her warily, accepting the comb which Graziella brought and the mirror she held.

'You're not at all like really. How old did you say?'

'Twenty years.'

'You see? Alice was only ten.'

'This was long ago?'

'Oh, yes, long ago. Goodness me, yes. You may not believe it, but I'm not very far off eighty.'

'Eighty? Ai, signora!'

'Yes.' She nodded complacently. 'Not very far off eighty. And until a few months ago I could walk—oh, I could walk a mile or so and hardly feel it. My husband and I used to be great walkers. Come along, he'd say, let's go for a tramp, and off we'd go. It was all country then, of course—Hendon, Golders Green, Mill Hill, all farmland. We used to take Alice picnicking. She loved to pick blackberries, her little mouth used to be all purple. You don't get blackberries in Italy, I expect.'

'Perhaps not, signora.'

Mrs Fingal hitched herself forward, her eyes bright. 'If you will fetch me the small suitcase from the top of the wardrobe

I'll show you a photograph of Alice. I did have it out but she put them away, for the dusting, you see. Then you'll see you're not really at all like. 'Graziella crossed to the wardrobe.' It's on the top, a dark-blue suitcase with my initials. It has all my personal papers in it.'

'I can see nothing here.'

'Nonsense, of course it's there. A small blue leather case with C.M.F. under the handle.'

Graziella got a chair and stood up on it. 'There is nothing, signora.'

'But there must be. It's always been there. Mr Evans put it there when I first came to stay. It has my papers and treasures. I got the cufflinks out of it, it was there then . . .'

She got down and put the chair away, dusting her hands. 'There is nothing there now, but there are many boxes, baggages, in my room. Perhaps it is there?'

'But why should she do that? It has only my personal papers in it. I used to look at it when I was in bed . . .'

'Perhaps to be safe. Perhaps not to make—pasticcio, too many pieces in the room.'

'But why would she move it? It has my personal papers in it, family papers and keepsakes. It has nothing to do with anyone but myself . . .' She was shaking, her hands crawling about the bedclothes. Graziella came to her and caught both of them in her own.

'Calm yourself, signora. Come now, be calm, lie back, take your breath. No one will harm your boxes. See, I will look in my room if it is there. You wait a moment, quietly, and I return. Yes?' She pressed Mrs Fingal gently back against the pillows. 'You wait quietly.'

In a minute or two she was back, the case in her hand.

'Eccol It is the one?' She laid it on the bed with a smile and Mrs Fingal clutched it. 'As I think, there are many and this I find. Now all is well? You are content?'

'It's very good of you. Thank you.' Her knobbly fingers felt round the clasps and handle.

'You wish to open?'

'No. No, I don't think I will, not today.'

'You will not show me the picture?'

'No, not today.' Her attention was no longer on Graziella, only half on the suitcase; she had withdrawn to some place of doubt which was-reflected in her face. Her head again began to shake a little.

'Va bene, signora. I put on the cupboard where you wish.' She made to take the case but Mrs Fingal grasped it.

'No. No, you must take it back. Put it back where you found it.'

'But you wish it here . . .'

'No, never mind. You must put it back where you found it.'

'But why?'

'I don't have to explain myself to you. Just do as I say, if you please. I don't have to explain myself to anyone, let me assure you. I'm perfectly independent, I can do as I please. Kindly take it back immediately.'

'But it is yours, signora!'

'I am perfectly well aware it's mine. Of course it's mine, it contains my personal papers. Now put it back quickly before she finds out.'

'Finds out what?'

'That we've touched it, of course!' She began to push the case away down the bed, shakily, her breath coming noisily. 'Go along, go along. Take it back. Take it back quickly.'

Graziella picked it up. 'Very well, if that is what you wish. You must be calm. See, I take the box now . . .'

'At once, do you hear, at once.'

'Si, si, pronto.'

Mrs Fingal sank back, her breath rasping between grey lips.

Her heart beat so wildly, it seemed to possess her whole body. 'I need—a pill.'

'Poverina—where?'

'Dressing-table.'

Graziella put down the case, went swiftly across the room and found the box, poured water, helped Mrs Fingal swallow. Then she held the dry old hand in hers, willing calmness into it. 'Now—see—you arc better, no? You must not excite so. I will do whatever please you. That is best, no? Come now, there, you are calm.'

'Yes—yes.' She shut her eyes.

'The pills should be close, here, where you can find.'

'She doesn't like it.'

'You should have water.'

'I knock it over.'

'So.' She released her hand, replaced the pillbox on the dressing-table, emptied the glass into the slop-pail. 'Allora, now I put back your box.'

When she returned Mrs Fingal was watching the door anxiously.

'See, all is well. Is back in my room with the others. And is locked, signora, I push to discover. And you have the key?'

'In my handbag.'

'So all is safe. You would like the handbag to make yourself content?'

'No. She doesn't like it. I muddle things about in it, all over the bed. But I know where it is, it's in the wardrobe. Or one of the drawers. Somewhere. I don't need it, now I don't go out. It makes litter, you see.'

Graziella sat down again, folding her hands in her lap, 'Perhaps when the sun shines you go out for a little? I take you perhaps, very slow, very gentle?'

'It's too cold.'

'When the summer comes . . .'

Spring. It has to be spring first.'

'La primavera . . .'

The door opened and Mrs Evans came in. 'Well, what a cosy picture. Having a nice chat, are you?' Her gaze took in the drawn curtains, the comb and mirror on the bedside table. 'Put those back where they come from, Gracie, and then run and put the kettle on, there's a good girl.' She came to the bed and tweaked back the covers. 'And I expect we need to go somewhere, don't we, before we have an accident.'

In the past months Mrs Fingal's legs had grown very weak. She could move from the bed to the chair only if she held on to the furniture. 'Be careful, dear,' Mrs Evans would say, beating up the pillows and clearing away all the oddments hidden under them, 'you don't want to fall and break your leg.' Trembling, Mrs Fingal would collapse into the chair, clutching her dressing-gown round her. To go along the passage she had to be supported and her feet would drag on the polished linoleum, her pounding heart make her so breathless that she would cling to whoever was helping her as though she really had lost all power to walk on her own. Mrs Evans supported her briskly, faster than the old lady's feet could move, would swing her smartly round, whisk up the night-clothes from the pinched buttocks and dump her down on the seat, the bathroom door only half-closed behind them by a shove of Mrs Evans's elbow. The outing was so nervously exhausting to Mrs Fingal that she postponed it as long as she could, often with disastrous results. 'You're a naughty girl, dear,' Mrs Evans would say, ripping the drawsheet off and dropping it on the floor, 'you shouldn't leave it so late. We don't want to get a bedpan, do we, for a bedpan really does mean it's all up, at your age.'

Dressing her was increasingly hard work, but here Graziella was allowed to help when she had been in the bungalow for a few days. Only with shoes and outer clothing; Mrs Fingal remained prudish about everything else. Graziella would guide the stiff arms into sleeves, do up fastenings, straighten collars and skirts, bring brush and comb, kneel and slip the knobbly feet into shoes. Then, standing, she would hold out her hands to Mrs Fingal, who shakingly reached up for them, haul her to her feet, her slender body braced, put her arm about the bent back, taking the weight on armpit and other hand, and slowly, steadily bear her on her tottering feet out and along to the living-room where Josh would rear up from behind his newspaper with a show of assistance that was always a little too late but which allowed him to put his arm round Graziella, stroke her shoulders, press her hand, brush his paunch against her hip as together they got the old lady settled in the rocking-chair. For these outings Mrs Fingal's eyes were bright and her heart beat in a different way, although just as uncomfortably. She had dabbed on some powder and put in her teeth; and once, when Josh was not there as expected, she walked by herself to the window to look for him. But after he realised that it was Graziella who escorted her in, Josh was always there.

While Graziella made her comfortable Mrs Fingal was often quite sharp with her. Her care was forgotten and she was impatient only for the girl to be gone, to leave her to the tête-à-tête with Josh, which he, sighing a little, shifting in his chair, smiled and jollied his way through, his thoughts elsewhere. When lunch was ready, it had been his job to get her to the kitchen table where they all ate. Now Graziella offered to do it, and Mrs Evans said, 'Well, dear, you could. It'd take a bit of the work off Mr Evans and me. Of course, the old girl won't like it. Hanging on Mr Evans is all she lives for.'

'For Signor Evans?'

Mrs Evans laughed heartily over the dishing-up.' She's a bit silly about him, poor old soul. It's a bit nonsensical really, at her age, but they get like that sometimes when they're old.'

'She has no family?'

'Not a one. All alone in the world till we took her in. The way I look at it is, you have to give a helping hand where you can.'

'She is truly ill?'

'She's frail. Her heart's not too good, you see, she might snuff out any minute. She's gone down hill a lot in the last six months.'

'It is the—spirito—that grows weak, to be in bed always. If you permit, I try to walk her a little bit each day. Perhaps her legs become strong.'

'You could try, of course—but I don't think it'll get you far. It only upsets her, you see, to ask her to do more than she's up to. And we don't want her upset, do we, for it brings on her attacks.'

'But to be always in bed when there is sun and not truly ill—is sad.'

'That's life for you, dear. I mean, we all have to grow old.'

As she fetched the old lady Graziella thought of her mother and grandmother, each of them looking ten years older than their ages in their widows' black but each of them full of vigour, to do or to speak. She drew Mrs Fingal's chair closer to the table and tucked the napkin gently in under her chin.

Thereafter, when they were alone, Graziella would encourage her. 'Come, signora, one little step. Do not fear, I will not fall you. Another—see, you are strong! Here is my hand—allora, avanti! That is good, good. It is the bed makes your legs weak. Together we make them strong, no?' Panting, groaning a little, Mrs Fingal progressed towards the living-room, one hand propping herself against the wall, the other clutching Graziella. 'See, each day one step more. What do you tell me how you are great walker? When comes la primavera you are again great walker.'

'What a beautiful word.' She halted, her eyes suddenly lifted from her feet and seeing Graziella. 'Primavera . . .'

'Si—la primavera when come all flowers and the sun and the young animals . . .'

'Primavera . . .' Dreamily she took another step, but her concentration had gone and Graziella had to support her rest of the way.

'Ah, hullo there! Here you are then, eh! Thought I heard you.' Hoisting himself to his feet, the newspaper behind which he had been listening for their approach dropped to the floor, Josh bumbled forward with his gestures of assistance. 'Here, let me—that's the ticket—easy now . . .', his hand covering Graziella's as he made to help the old lady, his nostrils quick for Graziella's warmth, his eyes darting from the nape of her neck to the falling forward of her breasts as she leaned down, the chain swinging with the small weight of the cross out of sight within her dress. 'There we are—all serene, eh? My word, you're looking bright this morning. Gracie taking good care of you, eh? Gracie's a great girl, eh?' letting his hand fall paternally on her shoulder, his whole body beginning to tingle from the palm of his hand that caressed the delicate bones through the wool.

'Prego.' Smiling, she moved to the other side of the chair to adjust a cushion. 'So, I leave you.'

'My hands are cold, Josh. Rub my hands.'

His eyes were still on the door Graziella had closed behind her. 'Mm? What's that?'

'My hands are cold. Rub them for me, Josh.' She stretched them out to him. Laden with veins, they shook a little.

'Mm? Ah, yes. Cold, are they? Poor old Cynthie.' Abstractedly he drew up a chair and sat beside her, enclosing one of her hands in both of his.

'They're always cold. Always have been. My husband used to tease me about it—cold hands, warm heart, he'd say, and he'd rub them just like you're doing. His hands were always warm, like yours. Warm as toast. 'Her fingers lay crooked between his plump palms but his warmth went right up her arm, right through her joints, easing her breathing and loosening her lips into a smile. That's better. That's nice. Cold hands, warm heart—that's an old saying, isn't it. Making the best of it, of course. That's nice. Men are always warm. I never needed hot-water bottles when my husband was alive. Warm as toast.'

He pulled himself together. 'Here, let's have the other one. That's right. Can't have you feeling cold, can we—that'd never do, eh?'

'I never feel cold when you're here. Josh, when the warm weather comes, will you take me little walks again?'

'We'll have to see about that when the time comes.'

'When the warmer weather comes—la primavera, they call it. Isn't that a beautiful word? There's a very famous picture called Primavera by a famous old master. They call it something else here but its real name is Primavera. It's in Milan. The sun makes such a difference. We'll go our little walks, won't we, Josh?'

'If you're up to it.'

'I shall be up to it. I was a great walker. We used to go for long tramps, my husband and I, all over the Downs and out into the country.' She lowered her voice. 'No need to tell her. She might not like it.'

'What, little Gracie?'

'No, no—*her*. Some women can't help being possessive.'

'You've got the wrong end of the stick there if you mean Maisie.'

'Dear Josh, so loyal. But I have my own ideas.'

He released her hand and gave her a pat on the knee before pushing back his chair. 'And some blinking silly ones they are too sometimes, old girl.'

Immediately she was flustered. 'Do you really think so? You're not cross, are you? Of course, she's a wonderful woman, and being a nurse . . .'

'She knows what she's doing, Mai does, never fear that.'

'I'm sure you're right. Men always know best about these things. Rub my other hand now, that's cold too.'

Indulgently he allowed himself to be wooed back.

Towards the end of the second week Mrs Evans said to Graziella, 'I don't want to push you, dear, but how's the job-hunting going?' She was making pastry with brisk surgical movements while Graziella peeled potatoes at the sink.

For a moment the knife halted, then continued above the muddy water. 'I am looking every day.'

'Answered advertisements, have you?'

'Oh yes, very many.'

'Shocking how they don't reply. I mean, you never get any letters here, do you, bar the ones from your family. Been to the Labour Exchange or the agency that got you your first place?'

'No.'

'Well, we've a saying here, Beggars can't be choosers. Go to the Labour Exchange, I should. They're bound to have something. It's off the Broadway, a sixpenny bus ride up the London Road.'

'I will do it.'

'It's not that I want you to go, dear, don't think that. But it's only a small place, and the four of us living one on top of the other—well, it gets a bit much, doesn't it.'

'You have been very kind.'

'Oh, I'm not asking for gratitude. We all have to help each other out when we can, don't we? But after all, your money won't last for ever, will it? And another thing, I think it un-settles the old lady having too many people about the place.'

'She don't like me?'

'It's not that, dear. It's just old people get funny ideas, and sometimes young people upset them. She's only living on borrowed time, you know, at her age. The least upset, a fall, anything, and she might snuff out like a candle. The doctor's warned us.'

'I am sorry. She seems only afraid.'

'Afraid?' Her floury hands and forearms stilled and she looked searchingly at Graziella's bent back. 'What d'you mean, afraid?'

'Afraid to be old—to fall, to do. When I help her, she can do. I think is not good to stay in bed so much.'

The flour was sifted again, the pastry lifted and turned and the rolling-pin began to move across and across it. 'I've been a qualified nurse for forty-two years. You're not telling me anything new. Of course there's disadvantages in bed rest, dear, but with a bad heart what's the alternative? As well as the risk of a fall and a fractured hip and I don't know what-all at her age. It's all very well for you young unqualified people to talk, but you haven't the knowledge. When they're as shaky on their pins as that poor old soul it'd be a full-time job to keep her ambulant with no accidents.'

Graziella had turned eagerly. 'Ah si, si—this I know. Forgive me, signora. I don't wish you angry. But is sad, to be old and lonely, not to walk. Surely is better try a little, hope a little? Already I think she is more strong.'

'How d'you mean, dear?'

'I hold her when she walk, I tell her she can do. I sit with her and she talk, we are friends.'

'Well, that's very kind of you, Gracie.' Clunk, clunk, the pastry-cutter stamped down in the firm floury hand, excising flat rounds of dough. 'But I'm not sure it's for the best. Apart from the risk of overtaxing her strength, there's the mental side of it. It over-excites her, you see, to encourage her to do more than she can. I've noticed it more than once in the last few days. She's been upset, over-excited. I've had to give her a sleeping-pill to get her off at night. Now that's not good, is it?'

'I am sorry . . .'

'Yes, dear, I'm sure you are. I'm sure it's the last thing you intended. But this is what happens when unqualified people try to take a hand. You leave it to me. I'm a trained nurse and I've had years of experience with old folk. I met Mr Evans when I was nursing in an Old People's Home, one of the old ladies was his grandmother. She brought him up from quite a young lad. Between you and me, his dad went off and left them after the first war. Never heard of him again. And his mother died of the 'flu. So his grannie brought him up, thick as thieves they were, real pals, but in the end she got senile, you see, and that's how we met. So you see,' she deftly set the pastry circles in the greased tart tin and dropped a spoonful of jam in each, 'we know a lot about old people, Mr Evans and me. You'd best leave the worrying to us and get out after a job of your own, dear.'

That afternoon Graziella took the sixpenny bus ride along the London Road as instructed, but she did not go to the Labour Exchange. There would have been no point, for she had no working permit and had never worked for a family in Westminster. For two hours she wandered round the shops, envying the girls their jobs, her face growing paler, her eyes smudged with fatigue, the belt of her skirt seeming after a while to be cutting her in half. She found a café and sat thankfully with a cup of liquid, tea or coffee she could not tell, and under the cover of her coat unhooked the fastening at the waist. At not much more than three months there was nothing to show; only she was aware of the stealthy swelling which made her waistbands so uncomfortable. She was lucky to have escaped sickness. Aunt Gina had been sick every morning until the fourth month, lurching greenly to the gabinetto, her hair lank over her face, while her husband,

Graziella's mother's youngest brother, still slept. She was lucky to have escaped that, especially now, in so small a house and under such sharp eyes. She felt tears rise up and clasped her hands quickly under the table . . . Remember, O most Blessed, Virgin Mary, that never has anyone fled to Thy protection . . .

'No,' she said when she got back to the bungalow, 'they had nothing. They will write me.'

'Keep after them, dear, I should. They'll soon have something.'

She lay down on the bed and thought of Mario and fell asleep, her long fingers over her hardly rounded belly.

She worked harder than ever to placate Mrs Evans next morning and went out after lunch, ostensibly to the Labour Exchange but actually to walk about the streets and sit for a while in a children's playground. She had given up hope of ever finding a Catholic church. The absence of Mass was heavier within her than Mario's child, but in these streets there were only the closed, scentless churches of the Protestants, she had never so much as glimpsed a nun, and she dared not ask a policeman and draw attention to her foreignness. God knew, she had much to confess, and knowing, surely He would forgive? On Sunday she kept to her room when the chores were done, to avoid attracting Mrs Evans's attention; but on Monday morning Mrs Evans said, 'Don't wait to help with the dishes, Gracie, you get straight down to the Labour Exchange nice and early. That's the time to get the jobs.' So she went out and took the bus and walked round Woolworth's and the larger stores again and did not know where to go or what to do. Stoically she began to walk back the way she had come, the London Road traffic thundering by beyond wider pavements as she left the shopping centre, the buildings dwindling to terraced villas, factory offices, little shops grafted on to the lower half of Victorian cottages, telephone kiosks and bus shelters. She was strong, but despair and exhaustion made her head spin. She went into something called Daisy's Snack Bar and asked for coffee. It seethed from an espresso. 'Something with it?'

'No. Yes.' She searched the ramparts of starch behind the glass case. 'This one.'

She found a coin and carried the food to a table. She was the only customer. She poured sugar into the coffee and resting her forehead on her hand, stirred the liquid absently, unable for the moment to consume it It was not yet noon. She could not return to the bungalow until the afternoon or Mrs Evans would be angry. If she were angry she would make Graziella go; even old Signor Josh would not be able to prevent it. And if Graziella had to go, where could she go to, without friends, without a working permit, with only a certain sum of money in her handbag, Mario's baby in her body, and in her head the plans for their ultimate future together, now plainly foolish, misconceived? There was always a solution. God did not permit one to despair. Nonna had not raised five children in the stony hills of Apulia, Papa survived war in Ethiopia and Egypt, Mamma kept hold of her family as the grey and then the khaki armies ground over them, out of despair. When she had broken the news to Mario that she was pregnant, his face had lit up like a blaze of fireworks, he had covered her hands and then her face and neck with kisses, before the shame and difficulties of the situation caught him. They had made their plan not out of despair but hope: to spare their families shame and to wrest themselves out of an economy which did not bloom for everyone in their own country. In England there was work. She first, before her family discovered her condition, to take advantage of old Signor Josh's invitations without waiting to arrange a labour permit, to stay as long as she could until Mario's permit could be organised and he could follow and marry her. They would have each other, work, a child. There must be no despair. But for the moment she could not summon her strength against it.

The man put coins by her plate. 'Change.'

'Ah gra—thank you.'

He stood looking down at her. 'Italiana, no?'

'Si.'

'Io egualmente.'

'No! Vero?'

'Si, vero. Carraro, Giuseppe Carraro.'

'Graziella Torroni.' They shook hands and Carraro sat down opposite her. He was a short, sallow man with sharp eyes, bitten fingernails, a grubby white coat, and carpet slippers. His Italian had an English twang.

'Where are you from?'

'Salvione, near Rimini. And you?'

'So many years ago, I almost forget. But never quite, eh? Urbino, that's where we came from—not far from Rimini, that's a coincidence. The world's full of coincidences. Back in the thirties my papa says, This is no place for little frogs with all these big black frogs croaking about, so he brings us all to England, Mamma, my three brothers and me, when I'm only five, six, I don't know. So what happens? There's a war and we're British subjects, so just when it's almost over I'm in the Forces, and back I go to Italy—comical, no? And what do I do? I meet a big fat Italian girl and later I bring her back here and give her three children and another in June. And where do I find her?' He struck his forehead with the heel of his hand. 'In Urbino. She's a cousin or something. I ask you, all those years and I have to go right back where we came from for a wife.'

'Urbino is beautiful.'

'Pah, what's in Urbino? Dead walls, fat tourists, empty bellies. Here we don't do so badly. Everyone has money—and the money calls the money, no? You have a fiancé?'

'Yes, in Rimini. Rimini.'

Why does he let you come to London all alone? Isn't he a man? I mean a compliment, of course.'

'Of course. There arc difficulties. It's not easy to find work unless you're a technician or in the tourist trade somehow— and even that fluctuates. Everyone told us there's plenty of work in England, so we planned to come here, marry and save enough to return and buy a business, a tourist shop, postcards, straw hats, sandals. At first modest, but with luck growing, more stylish, beach clothes, sweaters—I don't know quite, but I feel it I have the business head, he has the taste, perhaps. We would see.'

'And meanwhile?'

'Meanwhile . . .' She took a sip of coffee. 'To get a labour permit you must first have a job to come to. This is difficult for Mario, he knows no one, he's not a skilled workman only a clerk. So we decided I should come first.'

'And you work?'

She hesitated. 'I'm with friends.'

'There's always work for women. In hospitals, for example, they cry out for people to clean and cook.'

'I know. But I can't do that.'

'Why not? You're Italian, no? you can work like an ox.'

'I have no papers.'

'No papers? You mean, no permit?'

'No. I just came here, thinking I could be useful to my friends, that they'd be glad. But it's not like that.' Slowly the tears overbrimmed at last She wiped them away with her knuckles.

'Ai, mamma mia, you're a lunatic! Why didn't you get the papers? How did you think you would live, eh? You think the English give work to everyone who comes knocking? Pills, false teeth, operations they give, but work, that's different.' From near by came the wail of a factory hooter. Carraro got to his feet. 'You stay there, don't go away.' He opened the door

134

behind the counter and bawled 'Clara!' Movement sounded overhead and a voice answering 'Si, si, I hear.' Carraro busied himself with urn and stove. 'In a moment this place will be full, a madhouse, from the factory up the road. It's my living. You sit, we'll talk again later.'

The door was pushed open by the first customer and soon the place was a steaming, sizzling chaos. They slid into the narrow fixed benches flanking the narrow fixed tables, shovelling in the things on toast, the chips, the varnished rolls fringed with fat or cheese, gulping down the pale coffee and the dark tea or sucking from soft-drink bottles. As soon as one squeezed his way out another from the queue waiting by the counter and in the doorway took his place, while some ate from the counter and some took rolls and doughnuts away with them to eat elsewhere. They were young people mostly, talking at the tops of their voices, the boys with ear-long hair and big feet at the end of their narrow legs, the girls with casques or curtains of hair. The sexes did not mingle, although the boys sometimes whistled or called an invitation, which the girls primly rejected. It was food and a smoke they all came to Daisy's Snack Bar for, a sprawl and a natter before the hooter sounded again.

Behind the counter Carraro worked swiftly, serving, pouring, giving change, while in the alcove at his back Clara, his wife, fried and toasted in a haze of hot fat. All Graziella could see of her was a flesh-filled overall with dark crimped hair to the shoulders. Husband and wife did not speak, save when he transmitted orders, but worked with concentration in their separate spheres. Squeezed against the wall by youths who looked at her curiously, Graziella remembered the Albergo Garibaldi and the Signora examining every tray to see no portion was too big, and how so many English people passed compliments about the food, as though just because it was foreign it was good—Signor Josh had always done so, giving

135

if he could, a little pat to the waitress; Signor Billygoat, Francesca called him. She watched how the Carraros got through
their work, and when the rush had eased a little and no one
was sitting beside her she slid out along the bench and began
to clear the tables, carrying the dirty cups and plates behind
the counter to the stacked sink. Carraro washed what he needed
as the orders came; there was no time to do more.

At last the hooter sounded again and the remaining
customers clattered out. On the tables and on the floor they
left straws and bottle tops, wrappings from biscuits, cigarette
ends and empty packets, bits of crust, spilled sugar and gouts
of sauce. The windows were steamed up, the air stank of fat
and cigarettes. Behind the counter was a squalid seaside of
grease, crusts, dirty water and crockery. Clara turned and
sank down on a stool. Even without her seven months of
pregnancy she was fat, a large sad woman who held out her
hand wanly to be shaken. She gazed at Graziella without
expression as Carraro explained who she was, a smile passing
faintly over the plains of her face at the mention of Salvionc.
She hoisted herself to her feet and advanced to the sink.

'No,' said Graziella, 'I will do it.'

'You're a guest. Clara is used to it.'

'For a treat, let me. In gratitude for having met you.'

'Well . . .'

'I'm used to this work.' She took a cloth and tucked it into
her waistband like an apron. 'It's a pleasure to get down to a
great big sink of dishes again, like being at home. Sit, signora,
rest You've been on your feet a long time.'

Clara looked at her husband and he, after a moment,
nodded. Clara's eyes softened and she held out her hand again.
'Thank you, signorina.' With a small sigh she left them.

Carraro began scraping the debris into the dustbin.' I told
you, a big fat Italian girl, doesn't even speak English, not after
all these years—but good, a good wife, a good mother. The

kids are at school, the youngest's just started, he's five, and I thought he'd be the last. I should know better! Always children and none of them old enough to do more than eat. 'He raised his voice above the roar of the water running into the sink, wiping the counter and then going out to do the same for the tables.' When we first started, my brother was with me. We managed fine, everything went like clockwork. Then his wife wanted to move, right to the other side of London, half a day's journey. What can you do? He married an English girl, I had more sense, no? So he's in some factory now, like the cattle we've just seen, making bits of wire to fit into boxes. Is that a life for a man? We don't miss him too badly, Clara and me, with the kids at school she could manage. But now it's hard, she carries a lot of weight and her legs swell, poor little Clara. In another week, I don't know. I have to find somebody, no?'

It was nearly six before Graziella got back to the bungalow. Josh heard her footsteps and was at the front door almost before she was. 'We wondered where you'd got to.'

'I am sorry.' She stepped inside.

'Have you been all right?' He put his arm round her shoulders in real concern. She smiled up at him before moving free.

'Of course. I have work.'

'What's that?' Mrs Evans called from the living-room and Graziella went to the door. Embedded in her embroidery paraphernalia in front of the television set, Mrs Evans sat in Mrs Fingal's rocking-chair.

'I have work, signora. In a café along the London Road, Italian people.'

'Italians, eh? That's nice.'

'Oh yes. All day I don't speak one word of English, only Italian. Is like home! home!'

'You certainly look cheerful. The Exchange sent you, did they?'

'The Exchange? Ah si, they sent me.'

'I told you they'd find you something, didn't I?'

'We wondered where you'd got to, Gracie.'

'I am sorry. I start work at once.'

'So you're fixed up for a bit, are you?'

Oh yes. Every day from half past eight o'clock. But I will still be able to help here, signora.'

'Are you staying, then?'

'Of course she's staying, Mai.'

'I thought, if you will agree? At least for a little time more. I could pay now. You are so kind, so good friends.'

'Of course she's staying. We couldn't be without our Gracie, could we?' His hand pressed her waist.

There was silence for a moment, husband and wife regarding one another over Graziella's head. Then Mrs Evans picked up her embroidery once more. 'I'm glad you've found something. We'll have to see how it works out, shan't we.'

With a smile at both, Graziella slipped past Josh and into her room. Not waiting to take off her coat, she knelt by the bed to give thanks for the Carraros. They had even told her where a Caholic church was; tomorrow she would leave the house early and be absolved before work.

In the living-room Josh rubbed his hands. 'Well, that's good news, eh? An Italian café she said—fancy that.'

'I want her out of here before the summer.'

'But Mai, she'll be out of the house all day now.'

'I want her out of the house altogether.'

'You agreed she was useful. You agreed it looked well.'

'And so it did. But the point's been made. We want to keep to our time-table, don't we? With summer coming, the longer evenings, she'll be wanting to take the old lady out, get her mobile. She'll get her strength back. She'll even be offering to take her up to the Post Office and get her own pension, I shouldn't wonder.' She glanced sardonically at Josh, who looked uneasy. 'You don't think ahead, Boy. You never have. I'm sure I don't know what you'd do if you hadn't got me to look after you.'

'You're a wonderful woman, Mai. I know that.'

'God helps those who help themselves. There's just one or two more things that girl will be useful for and then she's out. We can't keep Cynthie for ever.'

Josh said no more. When Graziella came in presently to ask if she should start supper, he pretended to be so engrossed with television as not even to turn his head.

In Italian:

Rimini.

Graziella, my treasure,

With what joy did I receive your letter telling me you have found not only work but friends—for friends are perhaps even more important to your happiness than work, my brave little one. You don't say anything about your health—are you well, do you sleep soundly, and eat enough to take care of that fine fellow you're keeping for me? I worry about you in the cold and fog of England. How I wish . . .'

. . . It's good you have good news because mine isn't. Don't worry, my darling, all will be well but for the moment things are not satisfactory. I talked to my cousin again but without a sponsor even he can't get me a permit, and the man he thought might do it now says he won't (he lives in a town called Bradford which is far from London I think, so perhaps it's best). Time is passing and I (and the fine little fellow) can't wait too long to join you, so perhaps I must come on a Visitor's permit only and then try and arrange something—perhaps the Carraros could help? But at the moment I don't have the fare. My sister-in-law had to have an operation and I lent Ricardo some money, not so much for the hospital but for after when she ought to rest a little and eat well, also the children. So it will be another little while before I have enough to pay the fare. Don't be angry, you wouldn't want me not to have done it. Now that the season is almost starting —the first coach load of Germans arrived at the weekend—I shall be able to get evening work at one of the cafés after I leave the office, probably Saturdays and Sundays too, and this money will soon grow big enough to bring me to you. I go through the days in a dream of you, your tender eyes, your mouth . . .

. . . . . .

Always
Your Mario.

6

Mrs Fingal was not quite clear as to where Graziella had gone. It had taken her some days to get used to her being there at all (and she had never really quite understood who she was) and now she had to get used to her absence. As Graziella drew the curtains and helped her sit up, Mrs Fingal mumbled, 'You never come and see me now.'

'Signora dear, in the morning I come, in the evening I come. I am here now, no?'

'You never come in the daytime.'

'In the daytime I am working. You remember, I tell you how I work now every day with Italian people?'

'We're not in Italy.'

'No, signora—come, let me comb your hair—we are in England but these people I work for, they are from Italia.' Patiently she explained once more, and for a little while after she had gone Mrs Fingal had it quite clear in her mind. But gradually, as the solitary day wore on, it faded. When Graziella returned from work, brought in her supper tray, Mrs Fingal was tearful. 'You never come to take me for a walk now. You never help me walk.'

'Signora, I am not here. All day I am away at work, you remember?'

'So you say, so you say·'

'Someone else helps you walk—Signor Josh, no? or the signora?'

'No, no. No one comes. She keeps him too busy.'

'Come, sit up, eat your supper.'

'I'm hungry.'

Then eat—see, the bread and butter so thin.'

'I'm tired of just bread and butter. And the Ovaltine's made with water. I should like cheese. Cheese or a piece of fried plaice.'

'Signora, you would not sleep. You would have much bad pain in your stomach. This is best for you, Signora Evans says.'

'I can't sleep when I'm hungry.'

'But you have your pill. Is that which makes you sleep, not a full stomach.'

'So you say, so you say.'

'Come, eat.' She cut the bread into narrow strips and smilingly held one at Mrs Fingal's lips. Grudgingly, the old lady took a bite. 'There—is okay, no? On Sunday we have our walk again. We go round the room—three times, no?— and we go out of the door and down the passage and into the salotto. And if is nice day perhaps we go outside, a little way, along the path, no?'

Mrs Fingal shrank back. 'She wouldn't like that.'

'Why not? Is good to walk, to smell the air. Perhaps Signor Josh will help you.'

'No, no.' Tears filled the watery eyes. 'She won't let him.'

'Signora.' She laid her hand on the knobbly fingers. 'You must not think so. I have seen him help you.'

'No, no. Not for a long time. She's jealous.'

'Signora—she is a nurse.'

'She does it for the money. I've signed a lot of cheques—I'm independent, I don't need charity. We have so much in common, we used to sit and talk. Men are so different, so much more knowledgeable. One misses that—the talk and the getting taxis, ordering the wines, so much better at it, the little attentions. He hardly ever comes now.'

'But you go to the salotto, no?'

'No, you don't take me.'

'But someone takes you?'

'No, no. I never go now. I just sit in that hard chair while she makes the bed, banging about, so rough, like a hurricane. The bathroom, of course—but that wouldn't be him, naturally. She rubs me with something sometimes, but my heels hurt.'

'On Sunday you walk.'

And she did. But not into the garden, for it was one of those hysterical April days in which rain sluices the windows and beats down the early blossom. Instead Graziella supported Mrs Fingal to the boxroom. She sat her on the bed and showed her the pictures of her mother and of the Virgin Mary, Josh's snapshot of herself and Francesca which was still pinned to the window-frame. Mrs Fingal trembled and nodded, staring round the small room, her knees sagging. Even in the week that Graziella had been absent her legs had grown feeble again, and it was an effort for both of them to get her up and along the passage to the living-room, where Josh sat reading *The People*.

'Ah, hullo there—well, well, come to visit us, have you?'

'Is long since the signora is in the salotto?'

'Well now—a day or two perhaps. Legs a bit groggy now, aren't they, Cynthie.'

'With me she walk.'

'Ah yes, but you're something special, you are.'

Graziella pulled Mrs Fingal's skirt straight, propped a cushion more comfortably. 'Ecco. Now Signor Josh will talk to you till the lunch is ready.'

Under Graziella's smile it was Josh who got her to the lunch table and Josh who helped her back to her bedroom afterwards. Mrs Evans said nothing, merely observed; but Mrs Fingal babbled herself into a state of exhaustion from which she could hardly be wakened for her tea.

143

'You've overdone it,' said Mrs Evans at bedtime, 'I shouldn't wonder if you're not running a temperature. You can't play fast and loose with yourself at your age, you know. Here, give me your dentures. You'll feel it tomorrow, you know. You won't be good for anything tomorrow, not even if you have a good night. You'd best have two sleeping-pills, I think. Come along now, swallow them down like a good girl, I haven't got all night.'

Next day Graziella arranged with Carraro to have her half-day off on Thursday, when Mrs Evans would be out on her monthly tour of the needlework shops. She had already left when Graziella got back; Mrs Fingal was in bed and Josh asleep in his chair in the living-room. She washed and tidied herself, changing her work dress, which already smelled of frying fat, for a skirt and sweater. The skirt-band would no longer fasten and had to be latched with a safety-pin, but the sweater concealed this. She stared at herself in the mirror. She was pale but no longer sallow and had lost the dark patches under her eyes. Her face was softer, fuller. In the last week she had once or twice seen Clara's mild gaze reflectively turned on her. How soon before the signora, trained nurse that she was, would also begin to suspect?

Graziella went into the living-room. Spread round his paunch like a pink old baby, Josh slumbered. Sunlight lay across his shoulders and twinkled the stubble on his jowl. She began to tidy the newspapers that were dropped beside him, making some noise. He awoke.

'What? Eh? Who's this? Gracie?' He struggled more up-right. 'Gracie? What arc you doing here?'

'Is my half-day.'

'You never told us.'

She folded the newspapers neatly and laid them on the table. 'I am sorry if I wake you.'

'No, no—just dropped off for a minute. Thought I must be

144

dreaming, seeing you here. 'He was pulling down his waistcoat and trying to rebutton the top of his trousers, smoothing his hair, hurrying to get in dapper order.' Well, well, this is a nice surprise. Just the two of us, eh?'

'The signora has gone?'

'Yes, yes, she went off soon after two. She likes to get away as early as possible on what I call her visiting days. She's got a lot business to get through, you see. She'll visit three or four needlework shops, unload her tea cosies or doilies or whatever it is, get the account settled, have a chat and get the new orders, and then on her way to the next one. It may be a bus-ride away but she fits them all in somehow, providing they're all more or less in the same area. Then the next month shell go off in a different direction, you see, covering a different locality. She's a wonderful organiser, Maisie is.'

'She makes beautiful sewing.'

'She does, and it's all her own idea. She's full of ideas, Mai is, can't bear to be idle. She has this hobby, you see, so she makes something out of it. But sit down, sit down, my dear— you must be tired, standing about in that café all day. How d'you say it in Italian—stanco, that's it. Stanco, tired, eh?'

'Si, vero.'

'Stanco. It stuck in my mind, you see, because in English if you say someone's stinko, you mean he's had too much to drink, you see, so stinko, stanco, it's a kind of a joke. You stanco but I stinko, eh?' Joining in his laughter, she sat neatly in Mrs Fingal's rocking-chair opposite him. 'That's right, relax, take things easy for a bit. You do too much, you know. We've got a saying here, All work and no play make Jack a dull boy. Although I must say it seems to agree with you. You're looking bonny, Gracie, really bonny.'

'Grazie, signor.'

'Prego. That's the right answer, isn't it—prego? Prego,

signorina. Oh, it's a lovely language, Italian. And you're a lovely girl.'

'I am not special.'

'No, no, I won't have that.' He managed to stretch forward sufficiently to pat her knee. 'The moment I saw you, back at the old Albergo, I said That's a very special and lovely girl. There's something about you. And you get lovelier each day.'

'Each day you are more kind, you and the signora. Now I work all day I cannot help the signora.'

'No, no, my dear. It all goes like clockwork.'

'But some things I think do not get done. The old signora . . .'

'Don't you worry your little head about her.'

'But Signor Josh . . .' She gazed at him, her hands clasped in her lap, and he smiled fatuously back, hardly listening. 'I am worried about the old signora. She cannot walk now, only a little. Every day not so much, she lies in bed. No one walks her. When I come first, I walk her, slow, soft, every day a little more. Is good. But now I am at café all day, no one walks her.'

'She's getting old, Gracie.'

'So will we all get old—and lonely too, no?'

'Now, now, now—you don't want to be thinking things like that.' He hitched his chair nearer, which enabled him to take her hand. She allowed it to lie passively as he began to stroke it. 'Pretty young girls like you ought to be thinking about happy things, eh? romance, boyfriends, love. That's what everyone young ought to be thinking about, eh, Gracie? and that means the young in heart, too. That's what they call it, isn't it, the young in heart. We can't all be as young and lovely as you are, but we can be young in heart.'

'The heart can be young even when the body is old. The old signora . . .'

That's it exactly, Gracie. You've hit the nail on the head. The heart can be young even when the body's not quite as young as it used to be. 'Under his fingers the bones of her hand seemed to be sending tingling energy to every part of his body. Of course, Mai's a good bit older than I am. We met a bit late in life, you see, and it's never meant quite what it ought to to her, if you know what I mean. I've felt that sometimes, Gracie. Sometimes I've felt marriage hasn't been all that it should to a vigorous, full-blooded man. A man needs a bit of warmth, doesn't he, someone to cuddle up to, eh?'

Her other hand covered and stilled the frantic friction of his fingers. 'All people need love,' she said gently, 'the spirit as well as the body. The old signora loves.'

He stared at her, his attention caught through the haze of his preoccupation. 'The old signora? Cynthie?'

'Si. She loves you.'

He pulled his hands away and sat back in his chair. 'She's eighty.'

Graziella refolded her hands. 'In Italia we have many children. All are saying we have too many, we must do this, we must do that, but not so many children. Okay, perhaps is right. Many people is poor, there is not much money for clothes, for meat. But when they die no Italian people is alone. They have children. Signor Josh, the old signora is afraid to be alone. Alone, the fear grows—even I know this.' She looked down involuntarily at the small mound of her belly. 'Please, Signor Josh, be kind to the old signora.'

'Kind? Kind? Of course I'm kind.'

'I know. Is why I talk to you. Is not because you think I am pretty that we are friends at Albergo Garibaldi, that you receive me here. Is because you are kind—kind and lonely.'

'Ah, you understand that, Gracie—lonely. Maisie being older, you see . . .'

'You should have children, Signor Josh. I see you happy with many children, perhaps a daughter, to love and to joke.'

'I'd have liked kiddies, yes.'

'To care for you and fill your spirit quietly when not so young. The old signora too. Her daughter die many years past, a child only. Then her husband. All. Now she loves you.'

'D'you know something, Gracie? You're a very sweet little girl.'

It was she who now reached out and took his hand. 'Signor Josh, I know you arc kind. That is why I talk. Now I am away all day I think no one helps the old signora. She is alone much, in bed much, her legs and her spirit weaken, no? She is old, she spills, she drops, she is silly, but inside is young. All is gone—people, possessions, even fotografia arc put away now because of dust. She has nothing. No one comes. Signora Evans has much to do, she cannot spend time talking and helping. But you could do it. A little time here, a little there, that is all. Your arm, from her room to this. To sit with her. You don't have to listen, is enough for her that you arc there.'

He pressed her hand flat on his thigh. 'She's senile. She's not up to it.'

'Now she is not but soon again, yes. When I come she is weak, but every day I tell her, You can walk, I help her, listen to her, and she was better, no? Now I am away she is weak again, more weak because alone. No one comes. But you will come.'

Under her steady gaze he shifted. 'Well, I don't know. You make too much of it. Mai doesn't think . . .'

'The signora knows of the body but we know of the heart. You will do it?'

'Mai . . .'

'She will be glad. You also.'

'And you—what about you?'

'I also.'

He began to fondle her hand again, drawing it further up his thigh. 'You know what you are, Gracie? You're a minx.

A minx, that's what you are. You can twist me round your little finger, can't you? Right round your little finger. Can't resist you, can I? Simply can't resist you. You know how to get round me all right, you little minx, you? That's what you are, a little minx.'

His fingers were busy with hers, his face growing red. She got up, trying to draw away her hand, but he held it and reaching out, pulled her while she was off balance across his lap. 'Come and be cosy, Gracie. Come and say thank you to Josh for twisting him round your little finger, eh? What're you going to say to Josh, eh? Going to say thank you? Going to give him a nice little cuddle and say thank you?'

'Signor Josh!' In her efforts to get free she wriggled under his grasp and with a gasp he sank lower into the chair, holding her tightly, his eyes glazed, stretching himself beneath her struggling body. 'Signor Josh, please! This is not what is meant . . .'

'Be kind to me, darling, eh, darling? Just a little cuddle, darling . . .'

She twisted within his arms and he sank even further so that he was half lying in the chair while she, dishevelled and with her skirt dragged up, tried to get free. The door opened and Mrs Fingal stood clinging to the lintel, without her teeth, in a faded flannel nightgown, her bumpy feet bare. She looked at them, her empty mouth opening and shutting. As they struggled to right themselves her face began to pucker. She opened her mouth in a soundless wail and began to cry, letting go the lintel to cover her face with her hands. Her legs gave way and she slid cumbrously down on to the floor.

They carried her back to her room and put her to bed. They got hot-water bottles and brandy and Josh sat chafing her hands and rallying her in the way she had always liked so much. But there was no response. Limp, light, totally silent save at tirst tor the taint mewing sounds ot her griet, she allowed them to do whatever they liked to her. Her eyes were open but she looked through them. She had contracted herself to a point far beyond their reach.

Graziella was in tears. 'What must we do? We must fetch the doctor.'

'No, no. She'll be all right. Come on, Cynthie old girl, buck up now. Give old Josh a smile now, come along . . .' Loose as bones in a bag, her hand lay within his. Her mouth was so tightly shut that it seemed to turn inwards over her gums.

'Signora, please speak. Signora . . .' But the pale eyes roamed over the far corners of the ceiling, over the empty wardrobe top, over the window where blue-and-yellow washed sky showed that the rain was over.

'She'll be all right. She's overdone it, that's all. You're a naughty girl, Cynthie, getting out of bed on your own. See if she'll take some more brandy.'

'The doctor . . .'

'No, no. Mai wouldn't like that. We must wait till Mai comes back, she'll know what to do.' He stared across the bed. 'She's not going to like this. The old girl oughtn't to have tried to get out of bed alone, did she?'

'No.'

'She's not up to it. She's told her dozens of times, hasn't she?'

'Si.' She wiped her eyes.

'No need to say she got as far as the lounge, eh? No need for Mai to know that, is there?'

'No.' She turned away. 'When she returns?'

'Any time after five.'

'I will make tea.' She left him still chafing the unresponsive hand.

Josh was right. Mai did not like it. She stood in the hall taking off her gloves, unbuttoning her coat, while Josh faltered

his story, her face seeming to turn to granite. 'You old fool.'
She thrust past him into Mrs Fingal's room. Graziella rose
nervously from where she sat by the bedside, and Mrs Evans
stood glowering down. 'How long's she been like this?'

'Since four o'clock.'

'She's better now though, Mai. She's got more colour now,
hasn't she, Gracie?'

Mrs Evans thrust her hand down the neck of the nightgown
to seek the heartbeat inside its leathery cage. 'How d'you feel,
dear? You recognise me, don't you?' A small movement
indicated that she did. 'Can you speak, dear? Try and give us
a word so we know you can. Come along, dear, can you say
something?'

Faindy came the word 'Yes.'

'You can? That's splendid.' Her hand came out and firmly
sought the wrist, her eyes checking the pulse with her wrist-
watch.

'It was just a fall, Mai—nothing serious. She'll be as right
as rain tomorrow.'

She turned her stone stare on him, leaving the wrist. 'Did
she break any bones? You don't know, do you?'

'She didn't complain . . .'

'She didn't say anything, did she? She might have a broken
leg for all you know.' She stripped back the bedclothes and
began a swift examination of the small hulk exposed. 'She
seems all right. We've been lucky.' She pulled the clothes up
again and Graziella gently tucked them in. 'Well, we'll have
to see. Someone'll have to sit with her all night.'

'She'll be as right as rain, Mai. A good night's sleep . . .'

She seemed somehow to enlarge, although she stood without
moving. 'We don't want her going yet, do we? Use your loaf.
One of us must sit up.'

'I will, signora.'

'Very well. You and me can split duty. I'll get the doctor in

151

the morning. He won't want to come out now, it's too late for him.-

Graziella went for the doctor on her way to work next morning. The night had been quiet. Mrs Fingal had swallowed her pills and slept. Today there was more flesh on her face and she would speak a little to Mrs Evans although not to Graziella, whom she still refused even to see. She lay without movement and seemed very weak.

Daisy's Snack Bar opened at seven every morning to serve teas and buns to the factory workers before the hooter sounded at eight. Graziella did not start work until half past eight, when Carraro would have cleared and washed up, and on her arrival withdrew upstairs to a family breakfast, leaving Graziella to prepare first for the elevenses, which began at half past nine, and then for lunch, which began at twelve. There were cruets and sugar-bowls to replenish, walls to wipe down, rolls to split, butter and fill, potatoes to put through the peeling and slicing machine, half cook and drain for chips. A few van-or lorry-drivers came in for a cup of tea and would chat a little. They were mostly regulars, at first curious as to who Graziella was. She told them she was Clara's cousin. Overhead sounded the thump and clatter of the Carraro children, and a little before nine they ran down the stairs and out of the side door to school. Their father came back on duty between half past nine and ten. This morning he was morose.

That Clara! I don't think she's going to hold the baby another month. Always she's held on to them before, but this time. . . . 'Her legs swell up, she's got heartburn, she can't sleep, she says, when half the night it's I who can't sleep because there's no room in the bed. Mamma mia, who'd have a family!' He drew himself a cup of black coffee and drank it without sugar. 'And you! You look like a flea between two thumbnails!'

'I didn't sleep much either. The old lady was ill.'

'Bad?'

'I don't know. I sat with her most of the night but she wouldn't speak. The doctor's calling this morning. I think he should have been called last night but Mrs Evans was out and Mr Josh wouldn't do it without her.'

'She's the boss, eh?'

'Yes.'

'Show me a husband who lacks balls and I'll show you a domineering wife. Excuse me. But it's the truth.'

'An unhappy husband too, I think.'

'No. He's content. That sort of man, he's like a child safe in his mamma's arms. He doesn't want to run and shout, to fight to be a man, all he wants is to be a baby still. They should put the old lady in hospital.'

'Mrs Evans is a nurse.'

'So? Then why do you worry? Mamma mia, if I had a nurse in the house you wouldn't find me staying awake! Let her do the worrying. Here, sit down, for God's sake, and have some coffee.' He pushed her aside from the stove.

'I'd prefer milk.'

'Okay, milk, milk!' She poured a glass of milk and sat with it on the stool. 'You can't work all day and sit up all night, it's against reason. The old lady should be in hospital.'

'I think perhaps it would be better for her. I can't explain it, but I feel somehow uneasy.'

'Uneasy? My God, women!' Scornfully he began to clear the espresso machine.

'It's just a feeling. They take care of her, there's no one else, poor thing. But I don't know why they do it. They seem kind, they take care of her—but they don't care for her.'

I'll tell you something. The English are kind but they're not warm. Now us, we're warm, we have heart. The Italians will do very bad things but always from the heart, without shame, without pretence. The English don't do bad things but they're cold. You don't get to know them, never in a hundred years. But in all that time they don't do one bad thing. This is a land to be safe in—but also sometimes dead.'

She sighed and got to her feet to rinse her glass at the sink. And as she did so she felt a tiny drum-tap within her womb. She stood transfixed, the glass in her hand. After a moment it came again. Not wind or twitching muscle of her own flesh shell, but the small nudge of a creature that had come alive. Then stillness again.

In a dream she served the customers that began to come in. Daisy's Snack Bar full of people, the London Road full of traffic, the sky full of aeroplanes, the bungalow full of the Evanses and their prisoner, faded to unreality beside the realisation of her own fullness. Before, she had understood that she was pregnant, now she knew it. A personality more imperious than her own was now in being, that would shift and push against her till it broke out, and would become a man. She was dazed with the greatness of it, fatigued by the night and the stresses of what had gone before, and a longing for Mario came over her that was almost physical pain. She knew they should not have lain together before marriage and as a penance had tried to put all thoughts of it away. But now she ached for him, his thin cheeks and the sun-browned muscles of his wiry body, a body undernourished by poverty but made vivid and tough by the proximity of sun and sea, glowed before her eyes, could be felt under her hands, and the hungers of her youth could no longer be disciplined by reason or religion. She wanted Mario, she needed Mario, to share with him this creature that had started to flicker within her, his. To make more. To mate. To continue.

All through the morning she was consumed by this hunger. In the lull before the lunch time hooter, after they had swept the floor and wiped the table, she burst out, 'Signor Carraro, couldn't you send for Mario?'

'Mario, Mario? What Mario?'

'My Mario. My fiancé.'

He stopped what he was doing and stared at her, shoulders hunched in the grubby white jacket. 'Why should I send for your fiancé?'

'Because—oh, Signor Carraro, I need him so!' The tears gushed out She threw herself down on the stool beside the sink and covered her face with her apron. Carraro, immobile for only an instant, flung the broom on the floor and shook his fists at the ceiling.

'Mother of God, have pity on me! My wife upstairs having a baby, my silly cow of a helper downstairs having hysterics, twelve o'clock almost already, and what am I supposed to do? All I want is to run my business . . .' He advanced towards her, fingers bunched and gesticulating before his face. 'All I want is peace and quiet, a little calm, a little business. It's not much to ask. Holy Mother, I ask you, is it too much to ask!'

Drenched in tears, her nose running, she sobbed, 'I'm sorry, I'm sorry . . .'

'You're sorry! You're sorry! What am I supposed to be, eh? The priest, eh? The Welfare State, eh? Why should I have your fiancé? Answer me that. I've got you, no? Without papers, without permission, so I imperil my business, my wife and children. If the police come and say to me, Mr Carraro, this girl who's working for you, how did you get her, eh? Where's her labour permit, where's her insurance cards, how much do you pay her? And what do I answer? I say, Oh Mr Policeman, this girl is my wife's cousin, she comes for a holiday, she only helps out a little bit now my great fat cow of a Clara is having a baby . . .' His voice rose and he struck his forehead with the heel of his hand. 'And then they say . . .' His voice sank again, chillingly, 'they say, Very good, Mr Carraro, what does she live on, why don't your books balance, isn't it that you're paying her wages? What of her income tax, her insurance? And with my wife in labour and my three children crying for bread, I'm in trouble with the law! All this for you! It's enough, isn't it? It's sufficient, no?'

He sank down on a chair, staring at her with blazing eyes. She found a handkerchief and blew her nose. 'I'm sorry, I'm sorry . . .'

'Now. Let's be calm about this. You want me to have your fiancé, this Mario, no?'

'Not to have him—you needn't really have him. If you'd just send a letter asking for him, offering him a job so that he can get a permit . . .'

'And who would believe that Giuseppe Carraro of Daisy's Snack Bar, with a wife and three children—four children, Mother of God!—needs a waiter as well as a waitress?'

'Instead of me. I could leave. Or if not you, one of your brothers. . . .' Only to write the letter, it needn't be true. So that Mario can be here, so that we can marry . . .'

'No, no, no!' As his voice rose again, so did the factory hooter. He jumped to his feet. 'Enough. Do you hear? I've had enough. Dry your eyes and get on with your work. I've no time for romance and broken hearts, that's not life. Life is tea and coffee and baked beans and chips and Clara's heartburn. You understand me?'

Wiping her face, gulping the sobs back into control, she nodded. The door crashed open and the midday rush began. Carraro hardly spoke to her again all day.

After Graziella had left that morning Maisie had gone over Mrs Fingal carefully. The old lady was weak and silent but perfectly conscious. Maisie took her temperature (which was almost normal), gave her a bedpan, washed her and dusted her with talcum powder, combed her hair, cut her toenails, rubbed her salient parts with methylated spirit. When it was all done Mrs Fingal's temperature was up a little and she was exhausted, but she looked a credit to her nurse. She was given some warm milk and her pills, and fell asleep again immediately Maisie left the room.

Josh sat in shirtsleeves at the kitchen table with his second cup of tea. 'How is she?'

'There doesn't seem much wrong with her. We'll see what the doctor says.'

'Poor old soul.'

Maisie sat opposite and lit a cigarette. 'What happened?'

'What happened?'

'That's what I said.'

'Why, we told you. We heard a bump and went in and there she was on the floor.'

'*We* heard a bump?'

'Gracie did. She was in her room and heard the bump and went in. Then she called me. I was having a snooze in the lounge.' His candid blue gaze met and was defeated by her cold grey one. He shuffled, coughed, finished his tea.

'That's as good an explanation as any, I suppose. She's had a shock, that's clear. More likely her nerves are damaged more than her health. An old soul like her could make up her mind to go, you know, and we're not ready for that just yet, arc we?'

'Whatever you say, Mai.'

'Get yourself dressed and shaved and look respectable. The doctor'll be here before long. And when he's been, I want you in and out of that room making her feel happy, see? After a shake-up like that we'd better get organised.'

'Yes, Mai. I'll do my best.'

She got to her feet and put the dirty crocks in the sink. 'You'd better or we'll have wasted near a year's work, won't we?'

The doctor came, could find nothing especially wrong: weakness, irregular heartbeat, temperature and old age. In view of the latter, his brisk repacking of his medical bag implied.

there was little he could do. Rest, quiet, some more pills for stimulation—telephone if any change.

When he had gone Josh tiptoed into the bedroom. 'How d'you feel, Cynthie?'

She turned away her face.

'We'll soon have you back on form again, eh? Nothing much wrong with you, he says, just had a bit of a shake-up, falling like that. You didn't ought to have got out of bed, did you, you naughty girl.'

She did not answer.

'You're tired, I expect. You have a bit of a sleep, eh, and I'll bring you something nice for your tea. You'd like that, wouldn't you, Cynthie? Some nice bread and jam—or a biscuit, eh?'

She shut her eyes.

'That's right, you have a snooze.' He patted the shape of her knee under the blanket and felt it flinch. 'You have a snooze,' he repeated, and went slowly away.

When she woke up he was sitting by the bedside reading a magazine, which he put away as soon as he noticed she was awake. He brought her tea, called his wife and tactfully withdrew while the heaving up, the cold ugly rim, the stuffy odours of the bed were dealt with. Then he came back with a new hot-water bottle, and although she did not speak to him, did not seem even to look at him, he sat beside her again and chatted, teasing and rallying her, making little jokes, until presently she dozed again, lulled by his presence.

He seemed always to be there now when she drifted awake again, through how many days she did not know, but she knew when it was night because then he wasn't there, no one was there, not even the photographs of her mother and Stanley and little Alice and her sister, and it was dark save for the livid gleam of the street lights between the drawn curtains. The dark silence was split sometimes by the aeroplanes rising or descending at the fabled airport, and she knew what their sound was although sometimes she confused it for a moment with the shriek of a dog run over or the air raid sirens in the war or the whistling kettle when she had lived with Peggy in —wherever it was, she had mislaid the name. Sometimes when she awoke in the dark she could not remember where she was at all, and her heart would begin to panic and flounder until recollection came back to her.

Sometimes, in the evenings, she woke up to find that girl sitting there. She would not look at her or even hear her voice. The girl sat quietly, her face pale and pensive, looking down at her hands clasped in her lap. When she realised Mrs Fingal was awake she would smile and speak, leaning toward her, gently speaking, doing gentle things to pillows and bedclothes. But Mrs Fingal shut her eyes, shut her ears. The girl would subside again into her chair and at first she had cried, very quietly, only a sniff or two to give her away and the tears wiped away before they could fall.

But mostly it was Josh. Often when she first came back to consciousness she thought it was Stanley sitting here, dozing sometimes, dear fellow, or reading the newspaper; but deeply inside her she knew it was Josh, for vivid though her wanderings in the past could be, she knew them for dreams and that Stanley had been replaced by Josh with his silvery hair and his stout, tall, warm, firm body. Warm and firm—how firm he had been in Milan when they visited the Last Supper and the guide wanted a tip, all those beautiful little lambs on the walls, all pieces of coloured stone, and Stanley had refused to pay the man, who had been very abusive and Josh had just smiled firmly and bought her the postcards of those beautiful mosaics . . .

At first she had refused to look at him or speak to him, for if she did she would remember something which she could not survive. And survival was very important. Old, weak, lonely, longing to be finished with it all, tenaciously the young Cynthia still clung, shrunk but unchangeable, inside the husk. Let me give up, but let me not let go. She would not look at him nor listen, for fear of death. But she heard his voice through her closed eyelids, saw his kind, manly face as she listened, allowed his hands to warm her skeleton, until, at last, she turned her head and saw him again as he had always been, so kind, so manly, so protective.

But the girl she would not admit.

The weekend passed. The doctor did not propose to call again unless summoned. With Graziella out at work, Maisie took Mrs Fingal's small suitcase into the living-room and began to sort its contents. She knew what they were, of course, having been through them months ago, soon after Christmas, when the case was first moved out of Mrs Fingal's room. That was when she had transferred the handsome bed linen, towels and so on from Mrs Fingal's larger suitcase to her own linen cupboard, and thence to their own use. Once or twice at first Mrs Fingal had asked what had become of them, but she was soon silenced when Maisie had pointed out that they were too good for use on a bed where things were dribbled, spilt and wetted. It was, certainly, far more sensible to use up old, patched sheets and pillowcases, discoloured and thin. By now the old lady had forgotten she ever had any of her own.

Maisie sat in a shaft of sunlight, which struck pleasandy warm through her cardigan—a pity the weather couldn't have been like this for Easter. She replaced neatly the photographs, the bundles of letters, the boxes which had once held Stanley Fingal's tiepin, links, watch and cigar-cutter. She checked again the figures on the half-dozen share certificates that brought an income not large but adequate, and put them back. The document she wanted was beside them, and she took it out and put the case aside. For a moment she sat in the sunlight, skimming through the Will; it had been drawn nearly twenty years ago in favour of Mrs Fingal's sister Peggy, dead over three years now. Then, with the grunt which her solidity nowadays forced out of her, she got up and went into the kitchen. Over the sink she set light to the Will, holding it till the flames came too near her fingers and then dropping it into the sink to burn itself out. She flushed the ashes down the wastepipe, wiped her hands, lit the gas under the stew for lunch and was on her way back to the lounge when Josh returned from the Post Office.

'My word, it's lovely out this morning—a real touch of summer. I've a good mind to do a bit in the garden later on.'

'Come in here for a minute, will you.'

He hung up his hat and coat and followed her into the lounge. 'I got the form—one and sevenpence halfpenny it was.' From his breast pocket he brought out a printed Will form and laid it on the table, 'and there was two weeks' pension—we missed last Friday, with all the hullabaloo going on.' He put Mrs Fingal's retirement pension book beside the Will, and from his wallet took some notes which he handed to his wife. She counted them and put them away in the large handbag which stood beside her chair. He jingled some coins in his pocket. 'Shall I keep the change?'

'Yes, Boy, you can keep the change.' She opened the Will form and skimmed down it. 'Yes, well, you'd better start on this this afternoon.'

'Can it wait till tea-time? I'd like to get out in the garden a bit . . .'

'Yes, tea-time'll do. But I don't want you still talking to her about it when Grade gets back.'

'No, no, of course not.'

'I've seen to the case. One or two of the things had better go back, I suppose, just for the time being.'

'Right. Right, I'll get them.' Cheerfully he left the room,

returning presently with a pair of ivory-backed hair-brushes and a studcase, both monogrammed S.W.F., the tiepin, watch and cigar-cutter. Maisie took them from him, picked a silver hair from the bristles, and packed them into the case, placed the smaller objects in the appropriate boxes, and shut the lid.

'You can slip that in when she's asleep.'

'Right you are.'

'And start in on it at tea-time, eh?'

'Willco, willco!' Jauntily he saluted, two fingers smartly to his pink and silvery brow.

She picked up the pension book and the Will form and took them into their bedroom to lock them into a drawer. Then she went into the kitchen and beat up an Apple Snow for Josh's lunch.

When Mrs Fingal awoke at tea-time, he was sitting there as usual. The days were longer now but her room did not get much sun and a foretaste of twilight veiled the corners. She let herself hang in his warm hands as he hauled her up on the pillows.

'There you are, eh? Had a nice snooze? I'll bring your tea in a minute. D'you want to go?'

'No, no. . . .' Or had she? It didn't matter. What mattered was to keep him here.

'Want a comb, do you?' He combed her hair, inadequately. 'That's better. Have to make you look pretty, don't we? You look quite saucy with that blue nightie on.' It was faded to grey, but she preened in it. 'I'll fetch your tea. I could do with a cup myself.'

'You'll come back?'

'Of course I'll come back. Wouldn't miss having a cup of tea with my best girl, would I?'

Mrs Evans came back with him but did not stay. 'You're all right, are you? No bad turns?'

'No.

'No chest pains?' She shook her head faintly. 'Your colour's not bad. We'll see what you're like in the evening.' She tucked a cloth round her neck like a bib, straightened the sheets and went out.

Mrs Fingal plucked at the cloth, her eyes watering. 'I don't need this.'

'You do, you know. You might spill.'

'I shan't spill!' Pulling at the cloth, her hand struck his holding the teacup.

There now, all in the saucer! Better leave it, old girl.'

Weakly, she gave up. Her gnarled fingers sloshed more tea as they took it from him. He stirred it for her and she began to drink, noisily despite her first efforts. It was difficult to drink quietly without teeth.

While she drank, he chatted. She did not really listen to the words, only the voice, which sometimes seemed to be saying things said long ago by other people. Her feet were cold but they were a long way away, and when it got a little darker she would ask him to rub them for her. His warm, manly hands would rub warmth back into her, and meanwhile the tea made a warm path inside her so that even her nose felt warm.

'. . . when you've drunk your tea, that's what we'll do.'

She tried to remember what he had been saying. 'Yes.'

'I'll get it down, shall I?'

'Yes.'

She watched him get up and cross to the wardrobe, reach up and bring down her small suitcase. Mouth open, she watched, letting the saucer slant askew to spill tea on her bib. 'It's not there.'

'What isn't?'

'My My case.'

'What d'you mean, it's not there? This is it, isn't it?'

It was it. He put it on the bed and she could see quite clearly it was it. She touched one corner of it hesitantly.

'You're dreaming, old girl, that's what you're doing. Oh now, see what you've done!' He took the cup and saucer from her and roughly wiped her chin with the cloth before taking it away. 'This is your case all right—your box of treasures, eh? Go on, open it, and let's have a good old browse down Memory Lane, eh?'

He pulled it towards her and clicked it open. She had thought it locked—but then, she had thought it gone too, so she was obviously wrong about everything. Her fingers crawled slowly about the surface of the things inside, transmitting little shocks of memory: smooth ivory, the corners of envelopes, the clasp and pigskin rondure of a studbox, the dusty cardboard of mounted photographs. Sight and touch fused; recognition rushed in and she knew now every beloved object in the case, where bought, when given, who from and why. Letters, some of them black-edged, the folded paper with Alice's baby tooth inside, photographs, a curl of Alice's hair and one of Stanley's and a cap badge from the Great War, a menu from his office dinner spidered with signatures, some artificial Parma violets pinned to her coat for Alice's funeral and never again worn, Stanley's letters (so humorous, he should have written a book), school reports ending at nine years old, his cigar-cutter, not a bit tarnished, documents to do with investments . . .

She fingered them all, unable to stay for more than a moment with any, talking out her recollections—or perhaps only thinking them, for sometimes the room seemed silent except for Josh's encouraging exclamations. It got dark and he switched on the lamp. She was lost in joy, given back her past to spread out before Josh.

'I tell you one thing strikes me, Cynthie.' The serious tone of his voice halted her. 'It's not a very nice thing to say but it ought to be said . . .' You haven't got a Will.' She stared from him back to the attaché-case, then back to him again. 'All these letters and documents you've been going through, but I don't see a Will'

'I had a Will.'

'You don't seem to have got one now. Let's go through them again.' She relinquished the case to him, watching his serious face as he sorted deftly through her treasures. 'No, no Will. When did you make it, Cynthie?'

'I don't know.'

'It ought to be somewhere if you made it. Arc you sure you made it?'

'Yes.' But she was not.

'You don't think you just meant to make it? A lot of people keep on putting it off, you know, don't like the idea of it.'

'It was for Peggy.'

'Peggy? That's your sister, isn't it?' She nodded. 'Well, that explains it then, doesn't it? I mean, your sister Peggy died, didn't she? That's how you came to be with Lena first and then with us.'

Her fingers tightened. 'I won't let Lena have my things.'

'She will, though, unless you definitely say she's not to. She's next of kin, you see.'

'She's no blood relation.' She was beginning to shake. He laid his large, warm hand on her.

'Don't get upset, Cynthie. It's not good for you to get upset.'

'She's not to have my things.'

'Then you must make a Will saying she's not to. There's no need to get upset about it, you silly girl, it's easy enough done. I'll get you a form next time I'm at the shops and you can fill it in and we'll get it witnessed and Bob's your uncle. Easy as pie!'

'She's selfish. Hard and selfish. She'll sell my things.'

'Look, Cynthie, it's not going to happen . . .'

'She'll throw them away. She'll sneer . . .'

'Cynthie.' He leaned over the bed and held her firmly. 'It's not going to happen. All you have to do is make a Will, see, all legal and written out clear. Now quieten down, eh, else we'll have Mai after us. You lie there quietly and think who you want to leave your treasures to, and I'll get you a form tomorrow and you won't have anything more to worry about.'

'They're my treasures . . .'

'I know they are, and you want to leave them to someone who'll treasure them just like you do.' He gave her a squeeze and stood back, big and pink and smiling under his silvery hair. 'Now you lie there quietly and leave it all to your old Joshie, eh? Josh'll take care of you. You just think who you want to have them, and that's all you need do. When you've made up your mind, you just tell me and we'll get it all signed, sealed and delivered.' She lay looking at him, still shaking a little but trusting. He picked up the case. 'I'd best put this away, had I? Or d'you want it with you?'

'Someone might steal it.'

He wagged a finger at her. 'No one's going to steal anything from my Cynthie while I'm around. I'll put it back where you can see it's safe, eh?' He swung it back on top of the wardrobe. 'Well, I think I'll just stroll down to the corner and get a paper. It's a lovely evening. You'd like a look at the paper, I expect?'

'You'll come back?'

'I'll come back presently. You lie there quietly and think about your treasures·'

He took his hat from the hall and put his head round the kitchen door. Maisie was making a sponge sandwich. 'It's all right, Mai.'

'What?' She. stopped beating and raised her head.

'I said it's all right. Tomorrow or the day after, I should say.'

She smiled and gave a nod. That's my Boy.'
'I'm just nipping out to get an evening paper.'
'Rightio.'
He closed the doors on the sound of beaten batter and strolled, whistling quietly, through the late April dusk. With luck he might meet Gracie coming home. He didn't seem to have seen anything of Gracie since the old lady had her fall.

He did not meet Graziella, who came home a different way especially to avoid him. Since that dreadful afternoon, when she had so under-estimated Josh's ambitions towards her and it was the poor old signora who had suffered for it, she had spent such spare time as she had in her room. At first she had taken her turn by Mrs Fingal's bedside, but now Signor Josh was often there and in any case the old lady would not speak to her, would not even look at her. So now, after her tasks for Signora Evans were done, she withdrew to her room, to write to her mother and to Mario (although even this was difficult just now, for she could not risk their anger and grief if she told them what had caused the old lady's collapse), to read a little, and very soon to undress and go to bed, for unhappiness and the hard work at Daisy's Snack Bar were exhausting. Several times she had felt the creature shifting inside her, and she waited for it, loved it; it was company in the solitude of her anxieties. Nothing was right. She prayed a lot but no clarification came. To a situation of her own making, God was leaving her to find her own solution. This was just. He would guide her in the end, but she must work for it.

On her half-day, which was a Friday this time, she did not go back to the bungalow but to a cinema, seeing the main film twice so that she need not return before her usual time. She got back to lay the supper, to eat it submissively under Josh's banter and what seemed to her sensitive conscience Signora Evans's colder gaze, to wash up and tidy the kitchen.

As she was doing so the signora came back with Mrs Fingal's empty Ovaltine cup.

'When you've finished, Gracie, would you just come into the old lady's room for a minute.'

She did so. The old signora was propped up with her glasses on. Behind them her eyes were bright, there was colour in her cheeks, and her head shook a little. Beside the bed stood Josh, beaming modestly, holding a long sheet of paper. Signora Evans went forward and picked up a Biro from the side-table. 'We just want you to witness something. Just sign your name after Cynthie's done it.'

'Here you are, Cynthie. Here, half a tick . . .' He picked up the attaché-case, which Graziella had thought was kept in the boxroom, and laid it across Mrs Fingal's lap, then placed the document on top of it 'There, that's nice and firm. Write your name nice and clear, old girl, down here where it says.'

He pointed. Mrs Fingal took the pen in a hand that shook only a little, peering at the document and then up at Josh. 'Here?'

'That's right. Nice and clear, now.'

Mrs Evans stood the other side of the bed, her hands clasped. 'You know what it says, don't you, dear? You understand what you're doing?'

'Of course, of course.' She hunched forward and carefully, nice and clearly, wrote her full name.

'That's my girl!' Josh put his arm round her and squeezed her against his paunch, then pinched her flushed cheek. She lay back in rapture. Mrs Evans removed the document and pen, checked the signature.

That seems all right. Now, Gracie . . .' She left the bed and crossed to the dressing-table, placed the document on it and held the pen out to Graziella.

'What must I do?'

'Just sign your name here.'

'But why? What is this paper?'

'Just as a witness, dear. It has to be signed in the presence of two witnesses.'

'Why cannot you and Signor Josh . . . ?'

'Cynthie's been a generous, sweet girl, haven't you?' Josh at the bed was patting Mrs Fingal's hand.

Mrs Evans sent him a repressive glance. 'It has to be you and me, dear—someone not named in the document, you see. Come along now, just write your name here. It's purely a formality.' She indicated the place with her blunt forefinger. Graziella signed, scanning the paper to see what it was, but could read only a few words of the printed English before Signora Evans removed it. 'Thanks, dear, that's fine. Now you can run off to bed.'

For a moment Graziella stood, staring first at Signora Evans folding the document neatly, then at the bed, where Josh and the old signora fondled each other. The breath caught in her throat and she went swiftly from the room to shut herself in with an uneasiness that was swelling to fear; for one of the words she had been able to read had been Testament.

She did not know what to do. To whom could she convey this chill that made her sit shivering on the edge of the bed, her arms crossed over her stomach? The priest? She hardly knew him, an impersonal figure at Mass, an impersonal voice, not Italian, at confession. The doctor? She did not know him at all. And what would she say? An old lady, without family, looked after by an elderly couple, makes her Will. What more natural? Perhaps she leaves something (she surely cannot have much or she would be living in a different manner?) to the husband of the couple, and again, what more natural? Women need men to give to, and Signor Josh had been kind to the old lady . . .

Revulsion set her on her feet, pacing the few yards of space between bed, table and stored luggage. The luggage. Mrs

169

Fingal's small suitcase had been taken back into her room. Why? There remained here her larger case, which curiosity had shown Graziella weeks ago contained only shoes and a few cotton dresses. Beneath that was the trunk with different initials. Whose? Another old lady? Signora Fingal's predecessor, who had died? Died. Here, cared for by the Evanses.

What more natural? All people died, especially old ones. Nonna would die—please God with Graziella present with all the others round her bed—Mamma would die in time. And in time she herself, when the child now enclosed in her shivering body would be present and weep for her. It was natural, the shape of existence, the will of God, and better to die cared for and made happy even by strangers than alone in some institution.

Her longing for Mario was so intense that her flesh seemed bruised. She dared not write to him because if she did her anxieties would come pouring out and that would only make him suffer too. She knelt by the bed and bent her face to her hands.

There was an air of quiet cheerfulness about the Evanses that weekend. Josh got out in the garden, mowed the grass, staked the fast-growing plants, weeded—although that made his back ache. Mrs Evans started on an order for six embroidered tea cosies, all in autumn tints. Mrs Fingal lay in her bed, a shell from which the tide had receded. Sometimes she shuffled through the old magazines which sagged on the bedside table, but mostly she just lay, waiting for Josh to visit her; but he did not.

Graziella came instead. It was Sunday afternoon, when they all had their naps. Mrs Fingal drifted back to consciousness at the touch of two hands enfolding hers. Smiling, she opened bar eyes, but it was not Josh after all, but that girl, sitting on the edge of the bed. She tried to snatch her hand away.

'Signora, please hear . . .'

She removed her gaze to the corners of the ceiling and her attention as far as she could. Her hand she could not move, for Graziella held it firmly between hers, and could feel it tremble for escape.

'Signora, I am your friend. I wish you well only. You must believe me.'

There was no response, only another jerk of the dry old bones.

'Signora, I care for you very much. I think of you very much, like you are my own grandmother. I worry because you don't have no one to care for you and always I think how can I help this old signora?' No answer, only the gaze wandering over the room. 'Signora, is not right you have no one to know how you are. You don't see no one, you don't have letters. But when we are friends together you tell me you have relative, no? You lived with her, no? She should know how you are. Let me write her, signora.'

'Go away.'

'Signora, I beg you.' She leaned forward, her face delicate in its urgency. 'I am your friend. I want only to help you. We were friends, no? We talk together, we make walks. I don't want nothing from you only to help.'

'You're not my friend.' Mrs Fingal's gaze came to her now, indignantly.

'I am your friend, signora. I don't want nothing from you only to find someone for you outside this place. Is not good for you shut up alone here.'

'You're not my friend.' She managed to pull her hand away and hid it under the bedclothes.

'I shan't be here always. I have —I will go back to Italia some time and you will be alone. Is not good for no one to have news of you, if you arc ill or sad. This relative should know, should visit sometimes. Let me write her.'

'Mr Evans is my friend. Mr Evans is a very fine man.'

'But there should be relative also . . .'

'She's no blood relation. Nothing to do with me.'

'But you lived with her.'

'She's hard. Wrapped up in herself. She won't get round me again.'

'What is her name, signora? Let me write her.' But Mrs Fingal had closed up again. Her lips and her eyes moved, but not for Graziella. Graziella clasped her hands, leaning to the old lady in supplication. 'Signora, hear me. You are an old lady, all alone. When I first meet you, is in Salvione, you are on holiday, you are well and happy, no? With your relative. Now is only year later but you are here. You don't walk no more, you stay in bed only. When I come, you walk. Now, not. I don't know what is this paper you sign that I sign too. I don't know how you pay your food and bed, perhaps a bank does it. I don't know what money you have. But I think the Signora Evans knows and I think is not good that they are only people who have care of you.'

Mrs Fingal's gaze had come back to her, terrified. She had shrunk down in the bed so that only her head and shoulders were visible. She shook. 'You wicked girl!'

'Oh, signora, no!'

'You wicked girl! You think you can turn his head. Some men are like that, but Stanley never was. He had too much respect. You're jealous. You play on his weakness. Why did you come here? He's not concerned with you.'

'Please, signora, is not true . . .'

'You play on his weakness. You think you can get round him . . .'

'Signora, I beg you believe me, I don't have no interest in Signor Josh, none, none! He is kind, but to me he is like my grandfather. I come here because in Salvione he say many times I must visit him. Always he say it and I believe and I come.

Perhaps is bad that I come, perhaps is better I stay in Italia where my heart is.'

'You're after him.'

'Signora Fingal, I swear to you—see.' She pulled out the gold cross that hung concealed on the chain round her neck and held it out flat and warm on her palm. There was a locket beside it. To me Signor Josh is old. It is daughter he needs, not lover. He is silly sometimes but that I can't help. I have no need of Signor Josh.' The old lady was peering at the two gold emblems in Graziella's palm. 'You believe me. I know it. Dear signora, I am twenty years old. I have a fiancé in Rimini, soon we shall marry. His name is Mario, here is his picture.' She opened the locket and held it in front of Mrs Fingal. 'I shall be Signora Mario Antonelli and we shall have a child.'

'A child?'

'Si. A son. Always first a son.'

'Where?'

'Here.' She slipped the cross and the locket back inside her blouse. 'Soon. Mario will come, he will work. And later we go back to Rimini and have souvenir shop and we send you gifts from it and fotografia of our children. We will have four, but not too quick for first the business must be established, no? The son first and then the daughter. And I will call her Alice.'

'You're married?'

Joy at being at last able to speak of love made her forget for the moment the purpose of the conversation. She spoke of Mario, described him, told how they had met, sweeping Mrs Fingal along in a recital which bewildered but relaxed her. She did not understand half of what Graziella was saying, but the girl's radiance excited and pleased her, obliterating what had gone before. She lay staring at her, the girl's smile reflected in her own sunken lips, the girl's sparkle gleaming far back in her own half-comprehending eyes, her own heart and muddled wits responding with a strange, unsteady surge to the living hope of Graziella.

'Ecco! Now you know all.' But not of course, quite all. 'No one else I tell, only you because now you believe I am your friend, no? You believe it?' She laid her hand on the old lady's shoulder, and Mrs Fingal nodded. She hunched herself up a little, leaning towards Graziella, and whispered, 'You mustn't tell *her*.'

'You arc right.'

'She wouldn't like it.' She lay back again, looking uneasily about. 'She wouldn't like it at all. No children, you see. It makes a difference. She's not a generous woman. He suffers from it. Such a tender, manly man—one must make allowances. She would be very angry, you know.'

'We won't say nothing. Is our secret. And you will tell me the name and the address of your relative and I will write?'

She started fidgeting with the bedclothes, evasively. 'Alice.'

'Alice is your relative?'

'Alice was my little girl. I told you that.'

'I too will have an Alice, to remember her for you. Is the other name you must tell me.'

'Alice Cynthia Doreen—after Stanley's sister. Much prettier names than Lena.'

'Is Lena? Lena Fingal?'

'No, no, no I No blood relation at all. Kemp, of course.'

'I thought I told you, Gracie, I wouldn't have her upset?' Mrs Evans voice was steel. She stood blocking the doorway, wearing her mauve Sunday cardigan and heather-mixture skirt, grey hair neatly waved, grey eyes expressionless behind their spectacles.

Graziella jumped up and turned to face her. Mrs Fingal began to shake.

'She is not upset.'

'What d'you call that, then?' She jerked her head towards

Mrs Fingal. The old lady's face was grey and she had clasped her hands against her chest to ease the thunder there that made her gasp.

'Her pills?'

'She doesn't need pills. What she needs is leaving alone.' She came to the bed and brusquely felt Mrs Fingal's pulse, staring across at Graziella. 'You could kill her, you know. I warned you.'

'She was not upset. We talk . . .'

'So I heard.' She put Mrs Fingal's arm back, tweaked the bedclothes straight. 'You lay there quiet till Josh brings you your tea. You don't want another attack, do you?'

'Her pills . . .'

'They won't do no good. You lay there quiet.' She went to the door. 'You and me must have a talk, Gracie.'

She waited until the girl had gone slowly past her, then followed towards the living-room. 'In here.'

Silently Graziella obeyed. Josh stood looking out of the window, whistling and jingling the coins in his pockets. He turned as they came in and smiled uneasily between them. Mrs Evans sat down and studied Graziella for a moment in silence. The girl stood, her face pale but calm.

'Well, Gracie, I think the time has come for the parting of the ways.' Silence, save for the jingling in Josh's pockets.'We took you in when you arrived here without a friend in the world and although I won't say you haven't been useful, I can't say you've repaid us quite as you ought. I don't know your reasons for coming to us in the first place—I'm sure they weren't quite what you said, but I've never asked questions. All I have asked is that you'll do as I say about the old lady. I've said that not once but several times and you've chosen not to abide by it. Well, we can't have you pulling one way and me another, not in my own house. So it's best that you go.'

'Oh, come now, Mai, I'm sure Gracie didn't mean any harm . . .'

'Perhaps not, but the harm's done. I don't like people sneaking about behind my back in my own house. What were you after?'

Graziella raised her eyes. 'The old signora is alone.'

'The old signora is very frail and a bit weak in the head.'

'I do not think so.'

'She has her moments, of course. Old people do. She knows what she's doing some of the time, but mostly she lives in the past. It's kinder to let her be.'

'I do not think it is kind.'

'Well, that's where we have to agree to differ, don't we? I've been looking after old people all my life and you'll have to take my word for it. You were badgering her, asking her questions. Why?' Silence. She raised her voice. 'I said "Why"?'

'Now, Mai . . .'

Maisie turned on him. 'She was asking about Lena.'

He whistled. 'Lena, eh?'

She turned back to Graziella. 'I heard you asking all those questions. You were giving her no peace. To satisfy your curiosity I'll tell you Lena is the old lady's niece and they can't stand the sight of each other. She turned her out. If it wasn't for us, the old lady'd be in a Home. She doesn't want to have nothing to do with Lena, and neither do we. Is that clear?'

'Si, that is clear.'

'Well, then.'

'But is not right.'

'Not right? What d'you mean, not right?'

She clasped her hands tightly and raised her head 'Is not right that only you have knowledge of Signora Fingal. She is old and weak, si. But she is so because you do this. You treat her like she is dead already, you stay her in bed, you don't walk her, help her. Is not right no one but you has power with her. This Lena should know, she is family. . .'

'No one but us indeed! What about the doctor?'

'He sees only what is shown. He don't know how it comes like that. He don't know you make her sign a paper.'

Mrs Evans was silent, regarding Graziella with the grey immobility of a stone. Then she said, 'You'd best be out of here by supper-time.'

'Oh now, Mai—where'd she go at this time of the evening . . .?'

'I don't care where she goes. She can go to her Italian friends, foreigners all stick together. It's no concern of ours.'

Josh opened his mouth, then shut it again. He began once more to jingle the coins in his trouser pockets, looking uneasily from one woman to the other.

'Yes, I will go. And I will ask you where this Lena lives so that I send her news of her aunt.'

A dark rage seemed to swell Mrs Evans's face. 'Get out of this house!'

'If you arc not ashamed, you will give it me.'

'Now Gracie, that's not nice . . .'

She turned to him. 'Signor Josh, I ask you. You are kind, in your heart you are kind, I know it. You know what I say is true. Things are not good here. The old signora is helpless. She has only you. You she loves, you she trusts. I ask you to help her, to be kind, to love. Not love like you think, that you are silly with sometimes, but big love, from the heart, one soul for another. It is possible for you still, I know it, Signor Josh. Help this poor old woman whose heart is open to you. If you let her die like a frightened animal, you will be damned.'

'Get away, get away!' He flinched back from her, his face pasty, his eyes shifting towards his wife.

'Is true. You know it. This is fest chance for you.'

We've had enough of this. 'Mrs Evans's voice grated.' All

177

this Italian play-acting and hysterics. I want you packed and out of here, my girl, within the hour.'

'Signor Josh . . .' But he would not look at her, sidling into the protection of his wife's bulk. Graziella lifted her hands in a shrug. 'Ecco. I will go. But I will not abandon the old signora.' She turned to go.

'Just a minute.' Mrs Evans's voice was cool again. 'If you've got any ideas of making trouble when you leave here, I'd advise you to think again. Your own position's not too good, is it?' The girl was still. 'You're here without a labour permit, aren't you? I soon twigged that. Where's your national insurance, your P.A.Y.E., and that? You can't pull the wool over my eyes. You could get in serious trouble for that, you know, and the people you work for. And you never did have a job before you came here, did you, it was all a pack of lies, wasn't it, just so's you could sneak into this country and pick up some kind of a job illegally. The police'd be very interested in that, I can tell you. You could end up in prison, and so could the people you work for. And that's not all, is it? You don't want to draw attention to yourself now, do you, because you're in the family way, aren't you?' Convulsively Graziella crossed her arms across her stomach. Josh gave a gasp. 'I wasn't born yesterday, dear, no matter what you may think. I spotted your condition very early on, I can tell you. Of course, we don't know who the father is, do we?' Her glance rested sardonically on her husband for a moment. 'I suppose it's some Italian Romeo sent you over here to get rid of it.' She stood up slowly. 'Well, if you want an abortion, my girl, you've come to the wrong place. We don't do that sort of thing here, it's against the law. You'll have to get on with it as best you can—and don't let the Home Office find out, either, or you'll be in worse trouble than you are with the police. They don't like foreign girls coming over here in the family way and having their brats on the Health Service. Service.'

She took a step forward and Graziella shrank back against the door. Mrs Evans spoke pleasantly now. 'So if you had any ideas of making trouble, spreading wicked stories about me and Mr Evans and that poor old soul next door, you'd better think again, hadn't you? Because if I hear from anyone you've been telling lies about us, I'll go straight to the police about you, d'you hear? I wouldn't hesitate. You and that café proprietor of yours and his wife, you'd all be in serious trouble. And you wouldn't want the baby to be born in prison, would you?'

The two women stared at one another, the elder smilingly. Then Graziella caught her breath, turned and went quickly out to pack her things.

July

EW ANMIE,

Greenlea Avenue,

Ellbrook, M'sex.

Dear Lena,

Well dear, I am afraid this letter brings sad tidings. Your dear old Auntie passed away peacefully during the night. She had been failing for some time, the doctor had warned us she might go any time, it was her heart, it was just too tired to go on beating, and she had had a fall in May which the doctor said shook her up and did not do her any good. But he said of course she might go on for years. Well dear, that was not to be and I only wish I had had time to drop you a line earlier so that you cauld have paid a visit and tried to put things right between you. It is sad when they go without making their peace, death is so final, but you have nothing to reproach yourself with. She always was a wilful old soul, a real character, and ever since Christmas she had got some queer ideas in her head about you and would not have a good word. It is sad when you are her only kith and kin but there you are, old people all have their funny ways.

The funeral will be on Thursday at the Garden of Rest at 10.15 a.m. as she expressed a wish to be cremated and the Or has issued the Death Certificate with cause of Death Heart Failure, and Mr Evans and I do look forward to your being able to attend and come back here with us afterwards for a bite

180

and go through her bits and pieces. *The dear old soul did not have very much, as you know, but it is all locked up in her cases just as she left it. There are a few papers as well, but of course I do not know what they are and they will be left for you to go through.*

Well dear, I wish I had more cheerful news but it is not to be. At least you have the satisfaction of knowing she did not suffer. She must have gone in her sleep. We shall feel quite lost without her. I hope all is going well with you and that you are enjoying yourself at business!!

Mr Evans joins me in sending best wishes and condolences and shall hope to see you on Thursday.

Yours ever,
Maisie Evans.

7

Her hand on the gate, she halted.

'I keep telling you, we don't have to do this,' he said.

'We do.'

He shrugged and went with her up the path. 'You're crazy. I've married a mad woman.'

She rang the bell and they stood waiting, the carricot slung between them. Near by a blackbird whistled over and over again in the Sunday silence. From the airport a jet whined upwards.

They heard footsteps and the front door opened. It was Josh. For a moment no one spoke. Then: 'I don't believe it! Graciel Gracie, after all these months!'

'Signor Josh.'

He surged back. 'Come in, come in! And this must be— my word!'

'My husband, Mario Antonelli. And my son, Aldo.'

'Get away!' He peered at the sleeping baby, then gestured again. 'Come in, come in. My word, what a surprise!'

They manœuvred the cot through the front door and went into the living-room, Josh fussing round them. They got themselves seated, the Antonellis side by side with the cot at their feet, Josh facing them, rubbing his hands, beaming.

'Well now—my word! What's your news, eh? How've you been keeping? How old's this little fellow?'

'Six months, two weeks. He was born eleventh Septembre.'

'Get away! So you're an old married couple, eh?'

'Since July.'

'July, eh? And you're working here—er, Mario, is it?'

'Si, Mario.'

She sent him a darting smile. 'He doesn't speak English so well. I speak for both.'

'Ah—e —non parlo Inglese, eh? Molto—er—difficult?'

'Si, si, molto difficile.' A smile lit his watchful face like a passing light.

'He work at the Snack Bar.'

'What, where you were?'

'Si, si, with Carraro. He come, I go, he take my place. Carraro arranged it all, work permit, all. Is doing very well.'

'Well, well! Fell on your feet, then, did you, after all? I'm glad.'

'When I leave here, I go to Carraro. He make a big noise but he's a kind man.'

Josh's eyes shifted. He fidgeted with the buttons on his cardigan. 'I was upset about all that, Gracie. I felt badly.'

'I also.'

'Yes—well . . .' I've worried about you. You should have kept in touch.'

'I did not wish ever to come here again.' Her voice, her eyes were calm as she looked at him—a little stooped, a little more pouched, a little ruddier than he used to be. 'I come only for the old signora, to show her my husband and my child. She is here?'

'What, old Cynthie? No, no—that is, you see—well, she passed on, poor old soul.'

'So. She is dead?'

'Yes. Er—yes.'

'Since how long?'

'Well—let me see—July, it would have been. That's right, July. Nine months ago, very near.'

Graziella spoke to her husband in Italian, and he answered

183

her. His eyes, very beautiful, set in deep sockets, held a fire that made Josh uncomfortable.

Of what did she die?'

'Well—her heart, really. Passed away in her sleep. It didn't surprise us, you know. We'd been expecting it.'

'I also.'

'Yes—well . . .' He burst into activity. 'What about a cup of tea? You'd like a cup, wouldn't you—un tassa di tea, eh? Or coffee? It won't take a tick.'

'Thank you, no.'

'It's no trouble. We usually have one about now . . .'

'And Signora Evans?'

'She's fine, fine. Just popped out to post a letter. That is . . .'

Graziella stood up and Mario also. 'Is best we go now.'

'Ah now, Gracie, you've only just come. I've not had a chance to admire the son and heir!'

'He sleeps.'

'He's a fine little chap – how old, nine months?'

'Six.'

'Six—fancy! He looks like his daddy, eh?' He peered over into the cot where the baby lay like a peach in its wrappings, drenched in sleep. 'Fine little chap. I'd like to see him awake.'

'He was for the old signora.'

'Ah yes. Well . . .'

There was the slam of a car door, the gate, swift steps up the path; the key, the front door. Josh got to his feet, a mixture of emotions passing over his face. Lena came in.

As sight of them she halted. 'What on earth. . . . ?'

Josh moved forward. 'It's Gracie, dear. You remember me telling you about Gracie? And her husband Mario. They've paid us a visit.'

'I can see that.' Her stare took in Graziella, took longer over Mario, fell incredulously on the cot 'What's this, a baby? You didn't waste much time, did you. 'She threw her gloves on the table, undid the buttons of her moleskin jacket.' What brought you here this time?'

'They came to see Cynthie.'

They're a bit out of date, aren't they? Auntie died last year.'

'You are the relative of the old signora?'

'That's right. I'm her niece. Only by marriage, though.'

'I haven't had time to tell them all our news, Pussy.'

'Just like a man, waste time gassing and expect everyone else to know what he means. You'd better get on with it then, or I don't know what they'll be thinking.'

He put a tentative arm about Lena's shoulders and smiled winningly at the Antonellis. 'Lena and me arc married. Yes, we're man and wife. Still almost a bride, aren't you, Pussy— January it was, only three months ago. It seems like yesterday.'

She bridled, sending him a sleek, predatory look.

'But—Signora Evans?'

'Well . . .' He blushed, twinkled, looked at Lena, who tossed her head. 'It's all ancient history so it won't matter telling you now. Me and Maisie were never really man and wife. She had a husband living, you see. He didn't believe in divorce, one of those cranky religious sects, it's amazing how some people's minds work. They married before the war, he was a male nurse, a queer chap by all accounts. So when she began to get helpless, Lena moved in and—well, I persuaded her.'

Lena shook herself free and gave him a push. 'And a rotten bargain it was too, I can tell you. If I hadn't been fed up with Reading you'd never have got me.'

'Signora Evans is helpless?'

'Honestly, Piggy, you make a hash of everything. Yes, she had a stroke. And I'm Signora Evans, if you don't mind.'

'A stroke?'

'You know, paralysed. We had a row over Auntie's Will and she had the first one then. then.'

'She wasn't too bad, though, she could still get about.'

'The second one laid her out. It's a wonder to me she didn't have one before, all that weight she carried, you could tell she was the type.'

'Well, she wouldn't give up, you see.'

'She's had to give up now.'

'Come, Mario.' Trembling, Graziella bent to gather up the cot. Mario questioned and at her answer his face grew thinner and his eyes more fiery. He lifted the other handle of the cot. Josh put out a hand.

'Ah now, Gracie, don't go yet! Stay for a cup of tea.'

'We cannot.'

'We've not heard all your news, where you're living and all that.'

'Don't press them, Piggy, if they'd rather not. We've all got things to see to.'

'I never saw the little fellow awake.' He made towards the cot but Mario balked him. 'You must come again, Gracie— you must come again when he's running about, let him run in the garden, eh? It'd be nice to see a kiddie running about in the garden.'

'If we're still here.' Lena moved aside to let them get to the door, picking up her gloves from the table which no longer bore an embroidered runner, just as the chairs no longer bore embroidered antimacassars and cushions, but small square ones in bright modern colours. The curtains, too, were different, the ornaments cleared away, and Mrs Fingal's rocking-chair had gone. 'I don't plan to stick here much longer. I'd like to go somewhere a bit more lively while I'm still young enough to enjoy it, somewhere like Brighton or Clacton. Running round in the car, I keep my eyes open. Soon as I see a place I like, we'll be up and away and you can like it or lump it. I'm not keeping that millstone round my neck, thank you very much. We'd get a good price for this place, and with what Auntie left Josh. . . . I don't plan to stick here much longer, I can tell you.'

They were out in the hall, Josh rubbing his hands nervously. 'Would you like to look in on Mai? She's in Cynthie's old room now.'

'No, no!'

'Well—best not, perhaps. She can't talk, you see, although I think she takes in all that goes on, poor old girl.'

'Andiamo, Graziella.' Mario's voice was decisive as he held open the front door. Lena lounged in the sitting-room door-way, her bust cradled in her crossed arms. Josh fussed them out, venturing a pat of Graziella's shoulder, a hesitant hand, ignored, to Mario.

'Good-bye, good-bye—come and see us again. Ciao, that's it —ciao, Gracie—arrivederci, eh? All the best, all the best . . .'

His cries were blown away as they hurried through the gate and down the road. It would soon be dusk and ahead, along the London Road, the street lamps had come on, orange bars that set greenish shadows round their eyes and glittered the tears on Graziella's cheeks. Mario halted, and with his free arm pulled her towards him, holding her close, making a single closed unit of their two bodies linked by the cot, in which the child, touched by the cool air, was beginning to stir.

Presently he kissed her. 'Come now, enough. It's enough, my Graziella.' He found his handkerchief, wiped her eyes. Then they walked on towards the lights.

Printed in Great Britain
by Amazon.co.uk, Ltd.,
Marston Gate.